# THE CHEE-CHALKER

A full list of L. Ron Hubbard's
novellas and short stories is provided at the back.

*Dekalogy—a group of ten volumes

# L. RON HUBBARD

## THE
# CHEE-CHALKER

GALAXY
PRESS

Published by
Galaxy Press, LLC
7051 Hollywood Boulevard, Suite 200
Hollywood, CA 90028

Printed in the United States of America.

ISBN-10 1-59212-354-6
ISBN-13 978-1-59212-354-4

Library of Congress Control Number: 2007903547

# CONTENTS

# STORIES FROM PULP FICTION'S GOLDEN AGE

A ND it *was* a golden age.

The 1930s and 1940s were a vibrant, seminal time for a gigantic audience of eager readers, probably the largest per capita audience of readers in American history. The magazine racks were chock-full of publications with ragged trims, garish cover art, cheap brown pulp paper, low cover prices—and the most excitement you could hold in your hands.

"Pulp" magazines, named for their rough-cut, pulpwood paper, were a vehicle for more amazing tales than Scheherazade could have told in a million and one nights. Set apart from higher-class "slick" magazines, printed on fancy glossy paper with quality artwork and superior production values, the pulps were for the "rest of us," adventure story after adventure story for people who liked to *read*. Pulp fiction authors were no-holds-barred entertainers—real storytellers. They were more interested in a thrilling plot twist, a horrific villain or a white-knuckle adventure than they were in lavish prose or convoluted metaphors.

The sheer volume of tales released during this wondrous golden age remains unmatched in any other period of literary history—hundreds of thousands of published stories in over nine hundred different magazines. Some titles lasted only an issue or two; many magazines succumbed to paper shortages during World War II, while others endured for decades yet. Pulp fiction remains as a treasure trove of stories you can read, stories you can love, stories you can remember. The stories were driven by plot and character, with grand heroes, terrible villains, beautiful damsels (often in distress), diabolical plots, amazing places, breathless romances. The readers wanted to be taken beyond the mundane, to live adventures far removed from their ordinary lives—and the pulps rarely failed to deliver.

In that regard, pulp fiction stands in the tradition of all memorable literature. For as history has shown, good stories are much more than fancy prose. William Shakespeare, Charles Dickens, Jules Verne, Alexandre Dumas—many of the greatest literary figures wrote their fiction for the readers, not simply literary colleagues and academic admirers. And writers for pulp magazines were no exception. These publications reached an audience that dwarfed the circulations of today's short story magazines. Issues of the pulps were scooped up and read by over thirty million avid readers each month.

Because pulp fiction writers were often paid no more than a cent a word, they had to become prolific or starve. They also had to write aggressively. As Richard Kyle, publisher and editor of *Argosy,* the first and most long-lived of the pulps, so pointedly explained: "The pulp magazine writers, the best of them, worked for markets that did not write for critics or attempt to satisfy timid advertisers. Not having to answer to anyone other than their readers, they wrote about human beings on the edges of the unknown, in those new lands the future would explore. They wrote for what we would become, not for what we had already been."

Some of the more lasting names that graced the pulps include H. P. Lovecraft, Edgar Rice Burroughs, Robert E. Howard, Max Brand, Louis L'Amour, Elmore Leonard, Dashiell Hammett, Raymond Chandler, Erle Stanley Gardner, John D. MacDonald, Ray Bradbury, Isaac Asimov, Robert Heinlein—and, of course, L. Ron Hubbard.

In a word, he was among the most prolific and popular writers of the era. He was also the most enduring—hence this series—and certainly among the most legendary. It all began only months after he first tried his hand at fiction, with L. Ron Hubbard tales appearing in *Thrilling Adventures, Argosy, Five-Novels Monthly, Detective Fiction Weekly, Top-Notch, Texas Ranger, War Birds, Western Stories,* even *Romantic Range.* He could write on any subject, in any genre, from jungle explorers to deep-sea divers, from G-men and gangsters, cowboys and flying aces to mountain climbers, hard-boiled detectives and spies. But he really began to shine when he turned his talent to science fiction and fantasy of which he authored nearly fifty novels or novelettes to forever change the shape of those genres.

Following in the tradition of such famed authors as Herman Melville, Mark Twain, Jack London and Ernest Hemingway, Ron Hubbard actually lived adventures that his own characters would have admired—as an ethnologist among primitive tribes, as prospector and engineer in hostile climes, as a captain of vessels on four oceans. He even wrote a series of articles for *Argosy*, called "Hell Job," in which he lived and told of the most dangerous professions a man could put his hand to.

Finally, and just for good measure, he was also an accomplished photographer, artist, filmmaker, musician and educator. But he was first and foremost a *writer*, and that's the L. Ron Hubbard we come to know through the pages of this volume.

This library of Stories from the Golden Age presents the best of L. Ron Hubbard's fiction from the heyday of storytelling, the Golden Age of the pulp magazines. In these eighty volumes, readers are treated to a full banquet of 153 stories, a kaleidoscope of tales representing every imaginable genre: science fiction, fantasy, western, mystery, thriller, horror, even romance—action of all kinds and in all places.

Because the pulps themselves were printed on such inexpensive paper with high acid content, issues were not meant to endure. As the years go by, the original issues of every pulp from *Argosy* through *Zeppelin Stories* continue crumbling into brittle, brown dust. This library preserves the L. Ron Hubbard tales from that era, presented with a distinctive look that brings back the nostalgic flavor of those times.

L. Ron Hubbard's Stories from the Golden Age has something for every taste, every reader. These tales will return you to a time when fiction was good clean entertainment and the most fun a kid could have on a rainy afternoon or the best thing an adult could enjoy after a long day at work.

Pick up a volume, and remember what reading is supposed to be all about. Remember curling up with a *great story.*

—Kevin J. Anderson

KEVIN J. ANDERSON *is the author of more than ninety critically acclaimed works of speculative fiction, including The Saga of Seven Suns, the continuation of the Dune Chronicles with Brian Herbert, and his* New York Times *bestselling novelization of L. Ron Hubbard's* Ai! Pedrito!

# THE CHEE-CHALKER

# CHAPTER ONE

THE corpse was floating just at the bottom of the ladder where the dock lights reached thinly through the murky rain. The corpse was floating on its face, the way men will, and the back of the head seemed to move, though that was just the tide running through the hair. The tide had the corpse pinned against a piling so that the arms trailed out at an angle with the head and the feet curved in the same direction. The tide bubbles were full of phosphorus and lit it up all along one side.

Sven Nordsen had been drinking for about seven or eight hours and the quality of the liquor in Ketchikan had finally overcome even his strong stomach. He was so sick now that he was nearly sober. He stood on the Tamgas Trading Dock and wished he was back at sea in the *Mary D*, peacefully trolling for salmon with only a storm or two to worry about and maybe fog. Sven didn't see the corpse right away. When he did he leaned out and stared. Then he gave a shuddering kind of scream and went staggering up the dock to tell somebody about it. It was a somewhat wild night, even for Alaska, and so much had happened since dinner time that just one scream attracted no attention. Sven found Kelly, the night patrolman, and told him.

Kelly went down to the Tamgas dock and looked at the corpse. It was still there. Kelly flashed his light on it, looked at it for a little while and then said, "You go find Chief Danton, Sven. He's up at the Anchor."

Sven went up to the Anchor, more sober now, interested enough in his mission to avoid the three fights which lay in his path even though two of his friends were definitely interested. He found mild, serious Chief Danton.

"There's a corpse down at the Tamgas Dock, Mr. Danton."

"Who is it?" said Danton, finishing his drink.

"I don't know. Kelly said for you to come down."

"Have a drink, Sven?"

"Brrrrrrr! No."

"Never say I didn't offer you one."

"Well, maybe I better have one."

"Give him a drink, Morris," said Chief Danton, picking up his uniform cap.

"Something up?" said the barkeeper.

"Naw. Just a body down at Tamgas."

"Who is it?" said Morris the barkeeper, blowing his nose on his apron.

"I dunno," said Danton.

Sven watched Danton climb into his black slicker and leave. Morris set up a drink of rotgut.

"Takes the fog out of your bones," said Sven apologetically as he drained the glass.

"Who found it?" said Morris, faintly interested.

"I did," said Sven. "I looked down and there it was."

"Anything on him?"

"How do I know? I ain't got any love for hauling stiffs around. I tell you it sure was some shock to see it down there. Must've been in the water a month or two."

"Naw," said Morris authoritatively, "they go to pieces in a month."

"Damned if they do!" said Njiki the wolf trapper, down the bar. "I seen a floater up in Sitka one time that had been in the water two months."

"It's colder in Sitka," said Morris.

"Yeah, the hell it is. The water's warmer. It's closer to Japan, isn't it?"

A young man took a seat near Sven and threw down a silver dollar. He motioned Morris to fill up Sven's glass.

"You said something about a corpse?" said the young man.

Sven looked at him with suspicion. He was too well dressed and too neatly shaven to be an Alaskan. He had a peculiarly thorough way of looking at a person which wasn't polite. He must be a chee-chalker. Still he looked strong and it was better to be polite. Besides, he had bought him a drink, as Sven belatedly discovered.

Norton repeated his question.

"Yea. It was down by the Tamgas Trading Dock."

"Did you find it?" said Norton.

"Yah, I found it."

"Guess I'll go down and have a look," said Norton. He left his change on the bar and took up his raincoat. It was a nearly white trench coat with a wide skirt. Norton pulled

5

his broad-brimmed city hat down over his eyes and walked out. The rain was sweeping in regimental fronts along the dark boardwalks. The neon signs in the bars made little progress against the soggy dark. Norton walked down past the Sourdough Hotel and out on the Tamgas dock. A stiff wind was blowing up Tongass Narrows, blowing froth off the tops of the waves which were faintly luminous patches of white in the blackness.

Norton looked around. A light was on in the Fish Exchange and a lot of men were standing around in there. Norton pushed through the huddle at the door and came up alongside Fagler, the Federal marshal, who was talking to Chief Danton.

Fagler stopped talking and looked at Norton. "Hello, Norton." There was faint antagonism in his voice as though he resented Norton's butting in. The FBI was not too popular with the Ketchikan marshal, for it tended to override him in certain matters.

Norton looked at the corpse. It was stretched out on the floor, leaving a wide pool of water which ran out and mixed with the water streaming off the raincoats of the men who stood about it. The face was eaten away by fish. It was bloated and the flesh was gleaming white where it had been cut. Other places it was black.

"Who is it?" said Norton.

Fagler, the marshal, didn't answer.

"It's James England, the man who owns the radio station here." Chief Danton displayed the name inside the dead man's coat.

6

"Probably got drunk and walked into the water," said Fagler.

Bill Norton was only professionally interested. The FBI was not concerned with murder until it became part of other things. But Bill Norton didn't like the officious assurance in the marshal's voice. He bent down and turned the head to one side. There was a spot where the skull had been caved in.

"Fell and hit a piling before he went in," said Fagler.

"Yah," said Norton. "Every time I see a corpse pulled out of the water in this town it hit a piling when it fell in and broke open its head."

"It's easy to do," said a new voice, that of Thomas Hecklin, the local banker. He stood eyeing Norton from under the yellow brim of a sou'wester.

"That's right," said Chief Danton. "Besides, there ain't any call to stir up a lot of trouble with an investigation."

"Dead by accidental drowning," said the coroner, writing in a book. "Isn't that what you say, boys?" His jury nodded their heads.

Norton just looked around.

"Well? What would you do, then?" said Fagler.

Norton looked at the marshal and walked out. He walked out on the dock and stood there for a while letting the rain cool off his face. He hated being squeamish but he had never gotten so calloused that he did not get sick when he had to look at a drowned corpse. The nausea would come over him and stay with him for sometimes an hour. He looked at the patches in the dark made by the whitecaps and wished he was as tough as people thought he was. Or he wished that people wouldn't think he was tough so that he wouldn't have to be tough.

The men came out of the Fish Exchange and a wagon came for the corpse of James England. Paul Wagner came up and stood beside Norton in the dark rain.

Paul Wagner owned the Tamgas Trading Company and was a very important man in Ketchikan, even in Alaska. "Aren't you with the FBI?"

Norton looked at him from under his hat brim.

"Fagler said you were and I wanted to know what you thought about it. I'm Paul Wagner."

"Well?"

"I wanted to know what you thought about this. It is serious. James England was an important fellow to Alaska. His station up there on the knoll is Alaska's biggest and best. Now what's going to happen to it? I depend on him, or rather did, for my advertising. What do you make of it?"

"Make of what?" said Norton.

"Why, his murder."

"I thought they said it was suicide."

"They said it was accidental."

"I wasn't listening very closely."

"What do you make of it?"

"Why should I make anything of it? It's none of my business."

"I thought you were in town to look into his disappearance."

"Did you?"

"Well," said Wagner, his dark face turned full on Norton

now, "that was my impression. The Federal marshal wasn't making any progress and so I thought you had been sent down to look into it."

"Know anything about it?"

"About his disappearance?"

"Yes."

Wagner looked closely at Norton but he couldn't see through the rain and shadows well enough. "I know no more than anybody else. He had no enemies in particular and he was well loved."

"I heard differently," said Norton.

"No man is worth his salt who hasn't a few enemies," said Wagner nervously. He stayed around for nearly a minute but nothing more was said and so, uncomfortably, he went away.

Norton was glad he had gone. He wanted some more cold rain on his face. He wished corpses weren't a part of a lawman's business. At times like these he intensely regretted the small gold disc pinned to his wallet. That small gold disc sent him to such unseemly places.

Ketchikan, for example.

He looked at the rain and wondered that the skies were never emptied. A hundred and eighty inches a year was a tropical output with none of the tropical advantages. Of course it wasn't as cold here as it was in Juneau. Far north though it was, it was as warm through the winter as most of the US coastal towns. If only it wouldn't rain.

Bill Norton did not much like this country. He had been in it six months, most of the six spent behind a desk in Juneau, the last spent wandering around Ketchikan trying to get a lead on a sack of "snow" and Jerry McCain. He had found the heroin leading nowhere so far as he could discover. And he had found no sign of FBI special agent Jerry McCain. There was no more "snow." There was no trail whatever leading to the disappearance of his former boss. There was only rain. Rain and bars and drunken Indians and soldiers much drunker. Bill Norton, looking at the bobbing masthead and boom of a halibut boat tied to the Tamgas dock, was reminded of a gibbet.

Up the slippery boards skated a burblingly active young man, one of Bill's main responsibilities. Chick Star had just graduated from the School in Washington. Some clerk had sent him to Alaska on the first boat. Chick wore people out.

"What's the excitement?" said Chick.

"Corpse," said Norton diffidently.

"Aw, honest? Who, where?"

"England. Drowned."

"Gee! You finally located England? Gosh! Say, that's good work! Gosh, why wasn't I around?"

"If you'd stop chasing klootches you might get in on something sometime," said Norton, bored.

"Klootches," said Chick in a hurt voice. "I don't chase klootches. I can't stand the sight of an Indian. Why would I chase klootches?"

He was so earnestly involved, so gashed to the marrow, that Norton looked at him. Chick was six feet seven. He weighed two hundred and eighteen pounds. He ran into and knocked over things. He was twenty-three and serious. He was full of ambition. He polished his gold disc every night before he went to bed and carried his heavy Colt revolver to dances.

"If you don't you'll go nutty with this rain," said Norton.

"Oh, I like the rain," said Chick. "It's exciting. Things are dark and mysterious. Where'd you find England?"

"I didn't find him."

"But you must have," said Chick, gloatingly surveying his hero. "Was he stabbed?"

"He fell in and hit his head on a piling. The fish ate his face."

"Aw."

"Well if you can't take it you've got no business hanging around the Bureau."

"You're being modest," said Chick hopefully. "You found him and he was murdered and you know who did it."

"Sherlock Holmes doesn't happen to be even a faint relation of mine," said Norton. He slogged through the horizontal sea in the air toward bed at the Sourdough Hotel.

"Say!" said Chick, "did you see that?"

"What?"

"Those two men come out from behind that truck and turn the corner up there. They looked suspicious!"

"If they're suspicious you've given them plenty of warning with that brass voice of yours."

"Honest they did."

"Probably were having a quiet drink where their pals wouldn't ask for any."

Chick loped up beside Norton, splashing heavily through

the puddles like an overgrown tank and thoroughly spattering his despondent boss. Suddenly Chick threw out his arm to stop Norton and almost knocked him flat backwards on the slippery boardwalk.

"Look at that!" said Chick in what he hopefully supposed to be a whisper.

A young woman had come out of the door of the Sourdough Hotel ahead of them. The lights from the windows were not sufficient to show her features but they were ample to bring into silhouette the two men who emerged from an alleyway. The silhouettes swooped down upon the young woman and grabbed her. Hurriedly they led her straight toward the dock. They evidently did not see Chick and Norton standing on the walk before them for all was blackness in that direction.

"Take your hands off me!" protested a girl's voice.

"Come along," said one of her captors.

Norton was always faintly nervous when he was with Chick. He could never be sure what Chick would do. Chick would follow orders after a fashion—with a few "improvements" of his own—but when Chick had no specific orders, anything might happen.

Chick gallantly sprang forward. His first blow knocked the tough nearest the gutter sprawling into the street where he splashed and bounced and splashed again. Following up, Chick forgot the small detail of keeping his eye on the other man and was, in an instant beyond him, thus presenting his back. The arm of the second tough came up and went down. Chick curled into himself and before the sound of the striking blackjack came to Norton, Chick was a bundle of mud-stained clothes in the gutter.

Norton sighed. He stepped forward. The blackjack came down and the wrist swung into the crook of Norton's arm. Norton spun sideways to the tough. Out of the bearded face came a distorted yowl of anguish, cut by the muffled snap of an elbow. Norton caught the blackjack before it hit the sidewalk. Norton had no illusions. The tough was crumpling but one flip of the sap made the job complete. The other man was getting up and dazedly attempting to locate something to fight. He had his back to the lights. He saw the upraised blackjack and then he saw stars. Norton rapped him over the ear and across the nose for luck and then gave him a healthy kick in the ribs to see if he was still conscious. He wasn't.

Chick was moaning and the girl was crying.

"Shut up." Norton told the girl.

She looked at him through startled eyes.

"Ton of beef," grumbled Norton, picking Chick out of the gutter. "Stand up, will you?"

Chick's knees gave way and he sank upon the curb.

"Get up," said Norton. "Do you want to drown?"

The girl stood, paralyzed, it seemed, by shock.

"Well? Are you waiting for a fish derrick to come along and lift him?" said Norton. "Give me a hand."

Without taking her eyes from Norton she took Chick's arm and helped stand Chick on his feet.

"Now help me walk him into the Sourdough," said Norton.

She helped him walk Chick into the Sourdough. They

somehow got the weighty colossus across the lobby, a river of muddy rainwater in their wake, and up the steps. The clerk woke up and looked indifferently at them. He yawned and went back to sleep.

"Third floor," said Norton. "Bear up. Do you think I can carry him by myself?"

The girl put all the strength she could into boosting Chick up the stairs. The case was narrow so that they could not walk on either side of the injured gallant, but after much pulling and pushing and swearing by Norton they got him up to the third floor and down the hall to his room.

Norton shoved Chick onto the bed. "Get some water," he said to the girl without looking at her.

She stared at Norton until she reached the bathroom and only ceased when she had to locate the water tap and a towel. She came back and continued her hypnotized regard.

Norton pushed the wet towel over Chick's face and Chick tried to push it away. Norton felt the bruise and decided that the injury was slight. He decided that, not from any medical knowledge of fracture or concussion, but the belief that nothing short of a ton of dynamite placed directly under his feet could really hurt Chick.

"That's all," said Norton. "He'll come around."

For the first time she spoke to him. "I haven't thanked you for helping me."

For the first time Norton looked fully at her. She was a beautiful woman, that he could not deny. She was a heartwarming blonde in a land of brunettes. She was expensively and tastefully dressed and was certainly a lady, once more a rarity.

"Why?" said Norton.

"There . . . there's no telling what might have happened if you hadn't attacked those men."

"Yeah?" said Norton, his tone faintly ironic.

She frowned a little, failing to understand him. "But I truly appreciate it."

"You can beat it," said Norton. "If you please," he added remembering that she was, after all, a woman, and that he had to be polite.

"What's the matter with you?" she demanded.

"Lady, I don't happen to be as young or as foolish as my friend. Good night."

"You mean . . . you wouldn't come to the rescue of a woman?"

"Certainly. I'll rescue anybody if they need it."

"Sir, I do not like your tone."

"Lady, I neither know nor like your game. Good night."

"And what do you mean by that?" It was plain to see that her temper was delicately adjusted on a fulminate of mercury fuse.

"I mean you'd better paddle down and see if your pals have come to their better senses before they drown in this confounded rain."

"You are insulting."

"And you are obvious. Good night."

She slammed the door so hard that the walls went in and

out accordion fashion for seconds. Then she threw the door open and snatched up the purse she had left on the bed and slammed the door twice as hard. A moment later she opened the door a third time.

"I ought to scratch your eyes out!"

"I ought to hang one on your lovely eye for getting my young friend sapped. And if you open that door again, I will."

This time when she slammed the door, a chair fell over and a pane of glass fell musically out of the window to the street below.

# CHAPTER TWO

C HICK stirred fitfully at his breakfast and waited for the storm to break around his head. Norton did not seem ready to let it break for he sat askew on the leather seat in the Medlin Hotel Restaurant, looking sadly through the Venetian blinds at the sheets of rain which fell monotonously upon Ketchikan.

What a hell of a country, thought Norton. Ought to give it back to the Russians. Or the Tlingits. Or the weather. What wouldn't he give to be having this breakfast at Longprance in New York.

"Well?" said Chick, unable to stand it any longer.

"Well, what?" said Norton. "You got a clip on the noggin and it made you sick and now you are sorry for it."

"I suppose a gentleman was supposed to stand there and watch those lugs manhandle a lady," said Chick grievously.

"Who was manhandling what lady?" said Norton.

"You saw it," said Chick, glaring at his eggs.

"Saw what?" said Norton.

"Two lugs manhandling a lady."

"Where?"

"Aw, gee, Mr. Norton my head aches too much to get all balled up in one of your riddles. Those two guys would have thrown her off a dock or something if I hadn't stepped in.

And—" he plunged deeply and dangerously, "—I wasn't so far gone that I didn't hear you talk terribly impolite to that girl. She wasn't any common girl. She was beautiful and a *lady.*"

"Too beautiful," said Norton. "Entirely too beautiful for this Godforsaken country."

"I was right in doing something about it," said Chick defensively.

"About what?"

"There you go again," complained Chick. "And the way my head aches too!"

"If you'd keep out of the way of such childish brawls you wouldn't have headaches," said Norton mercilessly.

"Childish—Oh my head! Mr. Norton, have you no gallantry? Couldn't you see that she was being attacked?"

"All I saw was useless nonsense," said Norton. "Two men dash out in front of us. She comes out of the Sourdough. They attack her and we are supposed to attack them and get our blocks knocked off and then everyone will say it was a common street fight and bury us without musketry in a grave half filled with this damned rain."

Chick was gaping to the point of displaying his last mouthful of eggs. "You mean—that was a plot?"

"Call it a plot if you want. Personally I think somebody big time had better come up here and show these babies how to rub people out. All they can think of is splitting their skulls and dropping the corpse into Tongass Narrows where it very seldom ever comes up again."

"Gosh," gulped Chick. "Then—then England was murdered!

And they figured you knew too much so they staged a scrap to get you involved so they could rub you out—"

"Maybe. Maybe not," shrugged Norton. "But the lady of last night was a plant even you should have seen through, my thick-witted friend."

"Gosh. Then I did get sucked in, didn't I?" He worried for a while over his own stupidity and then came back, curiosity again working. "But why didn't they just shoot us in the back?"

"FBI men shot in the back are embarrassing. FBI men knocked over in a common street brawl where they have no business are subject to censure from the Bureau. You figure it out. I'm depressed."

"This has something to do with England's death. He was too influential. His broadcasting station was the only widespread medium of news in Alaska. He was murdered by somebody that wanted to shut him up." Chick gloated over his own perspicuity and forgot about his head for, in truth, he had been suffering more from worry than a chance concussion. Chick did not run well on worry. He was better running on the high wave of enthusiasm. "Somebody at that inquest figured you had something on England's death because you are the only smart law officer in Alaska. They wanted to kill you or something."

"Wonderful," said Norton, looking at the rain and thinking about the soufflés they served at Longprance.

"Then you did get something on somebody when you looked at England's body," said Chick, delighted.

"By the way," said Norton, momentarily abandoning

self-torture on the core of soufflés, "mail this when you are finished with breakfast." He handed an envelope to Chick.

"What's this?"

"That piece of evidence I took off England's body," said Norton, bored. "It has to go back to the Bureau."

"But you aren't supposed to keep evidence. You'll get in trouble with the marshal here," said Chick.

"They said it was accidental and closed the case. Besides, that is just a slip of paper with 'Montgomery and Roebuck' printed on it and some writing I can't make out. It isn't a bill but seems to be a note of some kind. Hence, I want to know what it says. Curiosity, that's all. Now get out and mail—" He changed his tone. "Sit still."

A man with bandages nearly covering his face, shaped to hold his nose in place, had limped into the restaurant and, failing to see Norton back in the corner, took a seat at the counter, his back to them. He was a heavily built man, as tall as Chick but burly. He wore a red cruiser coat and a sou'wester turned up in front. The way he squirmed around he seemed to be in pain.

"Who's that?" said Chick in a loud whisper.

"Shut up," said Norton.

"It looks like one of those guys that attacked the girl," persisted Chick. "But how did he get so bunged up?"

"Shut up," said Norton with an under-table kick.

"*Ooooof,*" said Chick and subsided.

A short while later another man came in by the door at the far end. The second had his arm in a cast. His face was pale beneath his black beard and his hat sat perched precariously upon the bandages which covered his skull. He took a seat beside the first one without saying anything.

"What happened to him?" said Chick. "That's the other one, or I'm blind and drunk. —*OOF!*"

Norton quietly finished his breakfast and then sat warming his hands on his coffee cup. He did not have long to wait for soon the young lady in question came up to the door of the Medlin Hotel Restaurant. However, she seemed to sense Norton for she turned to face him as she entered.

"Good morning," said Norton, getting up.

She seemed to be having difficulty in expressing her thoughts for they were obviously not friendly. She took the shaking-out of her green rain cape as an excuse to be silent.

"Nice even weather we're having," said Norton.

"I'm glad you think so," she stated. She seemed to be hanging between two decisions. In a moment she sat down and let Norton hang up her rain cape.

Chick looked at her in an alarmingly goggle-eyed fashion. He was trying to communicate that while Norton might be frosty he, Chick, didn't believe such things. However, the effect was merely gruesome.

"Something stuck in your throat?" said the girl.

Chick turned red and retreated into his coffee.

"I heard," said the girl, "that you are Norton of the Federal Bureau of Investigation."

"People are always hearing things in this town. The fact is doubtful."

"I have it on good authority," said the girl. "Permit me to introduce myself. I am Elaine Halloway."

21

"Pleased," said Norton disinterestedly.

"I have something I want to talk to you about. Is it safe to talk here?"

"That is all up to you," said Norton.

She glanced around but did not seem to take any particular notice of the two men at the counter not ten feet away.

"Mr. Norton, about two years ago my grandfather died and left me the ownership of the Halloway Halibut Fleet. I thought it was in good order and that it had been making money, but within six months the revenue began to fall off. I tried to get some reason for it from my manager here, Mr. Stoddard, but instead of information all I received was his resignation. Then when I came here a few weeks ago I found out that several loans had been made on the boats by Thomas Hecklin, the local banker, and it seems that I arrived just in time to see the loans foreclosed. There is something terribly wrong about all this. It leaves me stranded here in Ketchikan. I am sure there may be some justice in this land. How can it be possible for me to lose that fleet without ever having seen the papers on it?"

"That," said Norton, "is one for the Federal marshal."

"But Mr. Fagler tells me that there is nothing I can do about it. I thought if I found you and asked you, you might be able to tell me something to do."

"That's completely outside my line," said Norton.

"But . . . isn't there any law in this land at all?"

"Not enough to worry about," said Norton.

"But you are the law here. Alaska is a territory and under Federal jurisdiction and you are a Federal officer!"

"I am, perhaps, but you see, the Federal marshal is the one who is supposed to get concerned about fraud and such civil offenses. I am here to protect the government."

"But Mr. Fagler keeps putting me off. He doesn't seem to be interested."

Norton looked at her and sighed. Her gaze was straight enough and God knows her proud features were beautiful enough to turn any man's head. He checked himself smartly from an impulse to soften his tone and be kind and generous and understanding.

"Miss Halloway, Federal marshals are appointed because they helped somebody get into Congress or the Senate or because they have uncles and fathers-in-law that know people. But that's neither my concern nor my quarrel. That is the way the United States sees fit to run Alaska and I am not running the United States."

"You sound as if you were," she flared.

"All right," said Norton. "Get mad. But that's the situation."

"Cad," she stated.

"You know," sighed Norton, "you could make your fortune acting. Why worry about a halibut fleet?"

"Acting? What are you talking about, sir?"

"About acting," said Norton. "And lying and a few other things."

"You are insulting!" she soared. "I thought FBI men were supposed to be gentlemen!"

"So they are. If I weren't I would throw you out."

That raised her beyond the limits of speech and she stood there, tall and majestic, so angry that the silver foxes on her arm quivered in every hair. Her chair belatedly crashed on the floor, thrown back by her sudden rising, and scared Chick out of two or three hundred age minutes. For Chick had seen the two men at the counter get interested some seconds ago.

She spun about on a spike heel and left the place, the air smoking where she had stood.

The two battered roustabouts got up from the stools at the counter and loomed over the table. They were not pleased about anything.

"I," announced the black-bearded one, "I Russian Tarlof. I am tough. Last night you break my arm. Today you talk that way to Miss Halloway. Someday soon I put a fish fork into your middles and turn it around slow!" Deliberately he spat into the middle of the table and stalked out. His partner lingered long enough to nod once and decisively and then he too was gone.

Chick relaxed and mopped his head which had again begun to ache. "Gee! What is this all about?"

"Don't strain your brains," said Norton.

"But . . . but they got mad because you talked nasty to her and last night they were trying to beat her up— And she says she's in trouble and you say she's lying— Gosh. It's awful early to have all that happen."

Thomas Hecklin, dyspeptic and cantankerous and weasel-faced from trying to see through the bars of his bank into the pockets of his patrons, walked up to the cashier, a few yards from Norton, and paid for his breakfast.

"Good morning," said Hecklin.

"Good morning," said Norton.

Hecklin went out.

"Where did he come from?" said Chick.

"He's really a ghost," said Norton.

"Gosh. I wish somebody would tell me about things."

"I wish you'd keep your nose out of this and mail that letter."

Chick got up and gingerly put his hat on his head. There was a crash of glass and his hat soared over into the next booth. Chick would have stood there gaping at the bullet hole in the window if Norton hadn't nearly kicked his shins apart getting him down.

"Wh-what was that?" said Chick.

"A bullet," said Norton. "A bullet fired from a gun by somebody that is mad at us. If he hadn't forgotten the window you would now be a corpse. Bullets travel at considerable velocity and enter people and kill people."

"What are you getting up for?" said the shivering Chick.

"That guy is a mile from here by now," said Norton, prying the bullet out of the wall with his pen knife. "Pay the check and let's get out of here."

# CHAPTER THREE

FOUR days later, Norton stood before the long rows of bronze mailboxes in the Federal Building, pulling out his mail and quietly swearing, for the water kept running off his hat brim and down on the letters he was trying to organize. He ran out of filing fingers and moved over to the glass-topped ledge Uncle Sam had provided for his customers. Uncle Sam, however, had not provided much light and Norton was steadily getting into a bad mood when he heard the sharp rap-rap-rap of heels sixty or seventy feet up the way. Instinct made him glance in that direction and interest there held his attention.

Elaine Halloway approached her mailbox and stood digging through a woman's pocketbook debris to find her key. She was some time finding it and the interval gave Norton an opportunity to study her profile for the first time.

At first glance she looked fragilely beautiful, but a longer observation caught up the strength of her chin and the height of her brow, indicating a willful determination and considerable intelligence. She was, quite obviously, a woman used to luxury. Her clothing was silk beneath the rubberized silk of her rain cape. Black silk. Strange material for a woman to wear in Ketchikan where wool fabrics were almost wholly utilized.

She found her key at last and found only one letter in her box. Evidently it was not an important letter for she thrust it disinterestedly into her purse. She straightened her rain cape and zipped it up the front, her purse under her arm within.

Norton watched her, vaguely thrilled by her movements. She was like some luxurious leopard, easy but swift of action, posing her body indolently. And when she walked away, despite the rap of her heels there was a feeling about her of slow, boundless strength in reserve. Because she was tall, perhaps, she seemed to pace rather than walk. How little nervousness there was about her! Definite will and stubbornness, but nervousness, no. Norton had a sudden vision of her sheathed in silk upon the black spread of a divan, stretching her bent arm above her, exhibiting no excitement but languidly easing the vital tension which she radiated. A small, unexplainable quiver of excitement touched the hair at the back of his neck and made his fingertips unsteady on his letters.

He found, shortly after, that he had read the same address over about fifteen times without seeing it at all. He forced himself into casual action and thought once more. Odd, her effect upon him. No woman he could ever recall had had any upon him whatever. Was it because of his sudden realization that she was definitely a dangerous woman? Was it some eighth sense of alarm? Or was it positive attraction? Angrily he shuffled his letters together. He did not like to be affected physically or emotionally. He had always prided himself that his emotions were far, far away. That he could dictate the way he ought to feel about something and then feel that way.

And now that he was violently telling himself not to be in the least interested in that woman he knew he was disobedient beyond any hope of subordination.

He stalked out of the Federal Building. Or almost out of it. He was just about to push open the outward set of the double doors when he saw her again. She was standing on the walk talking to a man. Norton unreasonably did not like the idea. But neither did he want to intrude himself, which he would have done had he finished opening the glass door.

The drizzle made it hard for him to see the man's features beyond that the fellow was a native Indian or a Filipino. He had a yellow sou'wester pulled down over his brow, the straps of which were dangling. His short yellow oilskin jacket was too big for him, covering both hands, its collar swallowing nearly half his face. He had wool pants baggily thrust into black fisherman's boots.

Her conversation was brief, mainly of her own making, and Norton wished he could have heard it. She presently turned and proceeded uptown, picking her way through the puddles in the gravel street. The man to whom she had talked entered the Federal Building.

For an instant Norton had a full view of the face through the glass. Most Indians or brown people look much alike to white people, but Norton carried a full rogues' gallery of faces about in his head, that being part of his business. He quickly stepped aside, giving the fellow no view of himself, and went on out into the rain. He walked across the street and stood under the overhang of the Union Drug Company, waiting, a small excitement stirring up the bored lethargy into which he had fallen the last month.

A nose so smashed as to be no nose at all but a breathing place; an eye whose lid was split, revealing a streak of red and the inability of the Indian as a fighter; a weak but brutish mouth and a squatness of physiognomy peculiar to the Tlingit matched perfectly the picture of one George Fishcatcher, arrested by Jerry McCain, Norton's missing boss, on a charge of distributing heroin. But he was released for lack of evidence sufficient to convince a hostile jury.

George Fishcatcher came out of the Federal Building and stood in the rain a little while looking at the fishing boats in Thomas Basin. Shortly, having made up his mind, he went along the street in Indian Town on the water side, across Fish Creek and thence down the ramp to the Thomas Basin floats. At a good interval Norton followed him. George Fishcatcher shuffled along the greasy float to C Float and was there accosted by another Indian who held him in conversation a few minutes, made a sign of drinking and took George Fishcatcher aboard a seine boat and below.

Norton could watch the seine boat through a maze of trolling pole masts of other craft from the vantage and dryness of the green telephone booth at the bottom of the ramp. He did not find patience enough to wait very long for he knew that an Indian could take a lot of time over a bottle. He turned to the phone and called the Sourdough Hotel.

Ten minutes later Chick puffed down the ramp to Norton's side.

"You got a lead on England's murderer?" said Chick.

"Well . . ."

"Gee. Honest?" He looked at the boat Norton was watching. "Is he aboard that?"

Norton gave him a brief description of George Fishcatcher, adding, "He's a pretty bad fellow. When drunk, he'll kill on sight. He's already knocked off about thirteen men. He's drunk now and pretty soon he'll come ashore. When he does shadow him until he's someplace where it looks like he'll stay for a while and then phone me. But don't lose sight of him."

"Gee! It's dangerous!"

"Very dangerous," Norton solemnly assured him.

"You can count on me," said Chick.

Norton said, "The FBI depends on you, my boy." Then he shook Chick's hand and went up the ramp. When he got back to the hotel he took off his wet coat and shoes and lay down on the bunk, certain of a few hours sleep. Dreamily he wondered if George Fishcatcher had ever really killed anybody. Oh, well, it would keep Chick on the job.

Much refreshed, Norton took his dinner at the Medlin Hotel Restaurant, looking out at the rain with a sadistic smile. Every time a more vigorous gust swooped out of the sou'east and up the street, he smiled again. Chick had been feeling useless and in the way. But how proud Chick must be feeling now, with a dangerous criminal to watch. Norton could visualize him standing somewhere under a dripping eave waiting for a drunken Indian to stagger out and make way to another of Ketchikan's sixty-one bars.

Paul Wagner sidled up to the table, his dark, flabby face twitching on one side. Wagner had had a few drinks and it showed in the underlying pastiness of his flesh and the strange lack of color in his eyes.

"Been busy these days?" said Wagner.

Norton did not ask him to sit down. He did not like the fellow in the first place and he did not want company in the second place.

"Busy enough."

Wagner lurched against the table. "I bet you're gonna pick up the guy that got England pretty soon, aren't you."

"Wouldn't be amazed," said Norton.

"That so?" said Wagner instantly interested.

"Interested?" said Norton.

"Well, any man would be interested to see the man strung up that had killed his best friend."

"That isn't part of my business," said Norton.

"You just catch 'em for the hangman, huh?" said Wagner. He sought to make a joke of it, but there was more falsity than humor in his laughter. "Well, if you want any help, you just come down to Tamgas Trading Company and let me know."

Norton watched him walk away and noted that the walk was far steadier now than it had been before the brief interlude. The spoilers are still in Alaska, Norton told himself. Paul Wagner stood ready to strip any fisherman of his hard-earned profits, his boat or his household. Unlimited credit extended made Paul Wagner the virtual owner of the fishing fleet. A savory pair, Wagner and Thomas Hecklin.

The only other interruption was Russian Tarlof. Russian Tarlof was also drunk. A prolonged rainy period left the

Ketchikanians one diversion and, it seemed to Norton's distorted viewpoint, one only. Russian Tarlof's bandages were filthy and there was tobacco juice in his beard, matting it. Russian Tarlof stopped at the table and leered at Norton.

"You think you some fighter, hah? You think you can lick Russian Tarlof."

"Wouldn't be surprised, seeing that it happened once," said Norton.

"Yeah! You hit me from the back. Pretty soon I get well and I show you plenty."

"All right," said Norton.

"I am the toughest man in Ketchikan," proclaimed Russian Tarlof. "I eat people alive."

"Without salt?"

"Without sa . . . So! You make fun of Russian Tarlof, heh?"

"Might as well, for he doesn't seem to care how ridiculous he makes himself."

"How what?"

"Ridiculous."

"I look that up and if it is a bad word I kill you."

"It's a very bad word," said Norton.

Russian Tarlof went outside and began to stop people. Presently he seemed to forget about the insult and wandered off with his old pal, drinkward.

About nine Norton was lying on his bunk reading a murder mystery. During the last hour he had cast several glances in the direction of the phone, wondering that Chick had not reported. It didn't take an Indian that long to pass out.

Norton read another chapter and looked at the clock and

then again at the phone. Nine-thirty and no report. Well he'd wait another half-hour and then go down and try to trail Chick. Maybe the damned fool had gotten bored and gone to a movie or something.

Ten o'clock and a renewed shower of rain came around. Swearing at the Bureau for sending him Chick, Norton got into his white trench coat, shoved his revolver into its pocket out of habit and, pulling down his hat against the sheets of water, went forth upon the slippery boardwalks of the town.

Thomas Basin was well lit, the lights of its moored boats and those of the float reflecting badly in the rain-whipped water. Norton went carefully down the ramp. He did not suppose he would find Chick but before he began the round of the bars and the two movie theaters he had better make sure.

He went into the phone booth and found it empty—or nearly so. He almost turned back without seeing the hat. It was Chick's hat. Chick had worn its bullet hole proudly but now it had more than that. It had been thoroughly crushed as though stepped on in a struggle, leaving it a ruin. Norton lit a pocket fountain pen flashlight and went over the wet boards carefully. The rain had nearly washed away a long smear of blood.

Anxiously, Norton went over the other boards and found more traces. On the side of the booth was a large hand print, blotting out half the letter of an advertising sign. Disregarding the plea of the Boy Scouts and Sea Scouts—which was printed on the side—not to deface the booth, Norton ripped out the sign's glass. A fragment of it, striking the float, brought a query from the watchman's scow moored hard by.

"What's going on out there?" said the watchman.

Norton approached him. "Did you hear anything this evening? A fight, I mean."

"Well, yes, I reckon so. Two or three to be exact."

Norton looked at the glass and the state of the blood on it. "I mean the one about three hours ago."

"Oh, that one. Well, yes, come to think about it, it was a smart fight but it didn't last long. I was down looking at the light boxes on Float E and I guess I must have been slow coming back because it was all over when I did get here and then everybody was gone. Wasn't anything important, was it?"

"Did you see anybody around here?"

"There's lots of people around here comin' and goin'," said the watchman. "Now last night, for instance, there was fifteen or twenty people around the dock when that Siwash got drowned."

"Drowned?"

"Sure. Tied an anchor on himself and jumped off. Least that's what the cops figured out. Took them half an hour or more this morning bringing his body up. It's ten feet of water in here at low tide. Funny thing about that Siwash, though. He tied the anchor line around himself so he couldn't move his arms an inch. Must've been drunk, I guess."

"What about this fight you heard tonight?"

"Oh, there was a lot of cussin' and scramblin' around. No splashes though. If you're looking for somebody in particular I can get you a pike pole and let you poke around the bottom."

"Who owns that seine boat over there?"

"Which one?"

*"If you're looking for somebody in particular I can get you
a pike pole and let you poke around the bottom."*

Norton swiftly led the way to its side and read the name *Emilie Q.*

"I don't know," volunteered the watchman. "He's been here a month or two. Must be a hundred boats in here, you know. Can't know them all."

Norton stepped over the intervening boats and to the deck of the big seiner. The cabin door was ajar and he threw it open wide, looking down past the wheel into the combination galley and bunkroom below. There was no sign of George Fishcatcher or his friend. To be sure, Norton swung down into the big boat and looked into the forepeak. The place smelled of rotten fish and coal oil smoke and Siwashes. No one was aboard though all the lights were burning. However, that fact indicated nothing, for in this damp climate all boats used dock juice at a flat rate and kept their lights on to keep away the mildew.

A bottle was on the table, smelling of fusel oil and other Indian intoxicants. It and the other bottle by the bunk were empty.

Norton came back to the dock.

"You look upset, Mister," said the watchman.

"I'm peculiar," said Norton. "I don't like murder."

His tone chopped the watchman into silence. Norton went down the greasy floats and up the ramp. He had no way of knowing what had happened to Chick. It would be useless to consult the local police or the marshal—even dangerous. Certainly no one was angry with Chick. If this was vengeance then it was directed against himself, Norton. Maybe Chick was at fault; maybe Chick had stepped out and tried to take

George Fishcatcher and company into hand. If Chick was dead then he was down at the bottom of Thomas Basin and had been for at least three hours, too long to be saved, certainly.

On the slender hope that he was carrying evidence which might take him to Chick and determined to work on the assumption that Chick was alive no matter how violently the facts pointed towards Chick being dead, Norton returned to the Sourdough Hotel and went up to his room.

He felt guilty for putting Chick into that position, more because he had thought of it as a gag, letting Chick stand around in the wet. But he had supposed George Fishcatcher to be a harmless peddler about as dangerous as a dead sockeye.

The lawman side of Norton told him that he might be closer to solving the riddle of Jerry McCain's disappearance than he had been for a month. And thinking of both Jerry and Chick, Norton began to seethe. If he had had the responsible parties there in the room at that moment he would have outdone a Tlingit in ghoulishness.

He took Chick's celluloid hairbrush and dusted it to bring up the prints. Then he took Chick's water glass and got more prints. Finally he held the gruesome fragment of glass up to the light and studied it. He had to make this preliminary test in case they were Chick's prints, in which case they would be worthless.

The scar on the thumbprint of the glass and Chick's thumbprints on the tumbler and brush checked exactly. Angrily Norton threw the evidence into the wastebasket and paced restlessly up and down Chick's room. He could go to the police with this, but he was certain that anything they knew he could swiftly find out for himself.

George Fishcatcher was drunk. That liquor bottle on the table and the one by the bunk aboard the *Emilie Q* had been empty. A drunk Siwash, when he ran out of liquor, generally went to Indian Town to get more liquor.

Norton checked his revolver and slid it back into the pocket of his white trench coat. He went back into the rainy dark and strode toward Indian Town. He had no hope of finding his game, for if George Fishcatcher had indulged in murder that night, drunk as he was, he would have made himself inevident.

Two soldiers were rolling in the gutter outside the Northern Bar in Indian Town and a hiccoughing Siwash woman was cheering them on. One of the soldiers got up and began to kick in the other's ribs. Norton pushed through the crowd, thrusting aside the disinterested MP on the fringe. The Northern Bar had been nearly emptied by the fight but the crowd soon surged back in, three soldiers eager to buy the victor a drink and the victor fondly supporting himself with an arm about the shoulders of the fat Siwash woman.

Norton signaled for a drink when he could get the bartender's attention and when it was poured, said, "You know an Indian named George Fishcatcher?"

The bartender shrugged. "What's he look like?"

"He's a little runt with one eyelid sawed in half. He would be drunk."

"Ever see a sober Siwash?" said the bartender.

"Whozzat wans George Fishcatcher?" said a bleary voice up the bar.

"I do," said Norton, looking full at the Siwash.

"Wha' you say abou' George Fishcatcher?" said the Siwash.

"I want to find him," said Norton.

"You shaid he wash a runt."

"And if I did?"

"He my brudder. You can' shay tha' abou' my brudder." The Siwash pushed the people away from the bar and reeled up until he could blow his fetid, canned heat and fusel oil breath into Norton's face at close range. "You tak tha' back abou' George Fishcatcher, you damned whi' man."

"Where can I find your brother?" said Norton.

"Nemmine where you can fin' my brudder. You tak tha' back!" The Siwash swung. Norton backed up a pace because, for certain bacteriological reasons, he did not wish to bark a knuckle on him. The Siwash swung and missed a second time. So far nobody had paid much attention.

Norton was out of temper. "Listen. Where can I find your brother?"

"You tak tha' back, I shay!" And the Siwash picked up a bottle by the neck and struck with it.

Norton shattered the weapon with his revolver muzzle. In the second sweep he brought the barrel down over the Siwash's ear. Alaskan fighting had been taught Norton in just six months for he had seen too much of it not to appreciate that the Marquis of Queensberry ceased to rule north of thirty-eight. The Siwash was still clawing at him for he had not struck hard. Now Norton did strike, across the bridge of the man's nose, which caved in and gave forth a fountain of gore. Three of the Siwash's friends instantly considered it their business for they had not seen Norton's gun and thought it a blackjack. One hauled at Norton from behind and got a heel in his groin. Another lunged from the right and caught the pistol barrel in his solar plexus and again in his jaw before he went down.

The place was abruptly a screaming madhouse, for the fight had become numerous enough to affect everybody. Soldiers began slugging wildly at any target in sight. Bottles crashed on defenseless skulls. Men went down and got their faces kicked in. Teeth flew. Brass knuckles glittered.

Norton went over the bar and landed on top of the cowering bartender. Seeing somebody escape, half a dozen men tried to reach over and get at him. Norton pitched all the bottles in sight at them, meanwhile making his way down the inside of the bar. Discouraged, the men forgot about him.

Norton made his way around the fringe of the crowd, crowning anyone who swung at him and swinging them back into the melee where they got swung at anew for running into somebody. He was almost to the door when he saw George Fishcatcher.

Uttering Tlingit warwhoops, the Siwash was waving a glass at the fight and swinging at empty air, all the while seated in the furthest booth from the door. The man with him was sprawled out, head on the table, obliviously sick.

Norton reached out and got George Fishcatcher by the throat and yanked him out of the booth. George Fishcatcher tried to bite and kick and made a final contact with his glass on Norton's face. Norton gave him a knee in the groin which relaxed the Siwash a trifle and then got him around the throat in such a way that George Fishcatcher, if he kept struggling, would earn himself a broken neck in one direction and a strangling in the other. The hold was messy, for George was already bleeding from a laid-open scalp.

Hammering his prisoner now and then in the kidney with his revolver barrel, Norton finally got him through the battle and into the street. Norton was not much touched in the passage, for all thrown missiles, flailing chairs and brass knuckles had to hit George Fishcatcher before they could get to Norton, who was careful to keep the wall between himself and the war.

He got his game outside in time to see Kelly and Chief Danton walk into the Northern Bar, swinging night sticks indiscriminately. Most of the combatants were worn out by this time and so it was not difficult to stop the battle.

On the walk which departed from Stedman Street and ran darkly up beside roaring Fish Creek, Norton found a rain spout which was gushing icy water. The rain had not been enough to bring George Fishcatcher around. When it was either come to or drown, George Fishcatcher came to.

"What boat are you on?" demanded Norton.

"Ughlub," said George Fishcatcher.

"What boat are you on?" repeated Norton.

"Ooohch, I am sooo sick. Ughlub! Glack!"

Norton let his head out from under the gushing rain spout. "What boat, damn you?"

"Ughlub! Glag, woch!" agonized George Fishcatcher. "I'b drownb!"

"Drown and be damned," said Norton. "What boat?"

"Roj . . . Roger . . . Ubglooooooo . . . Roger Halloway!"

"Did you see anything of a big white man down on the Thomas Basin float earlier this evening?"

"Glob, bloourk. Ooooooooo! Dob. Pleab dob! I'b drownbdig!"

Norton kicked him in the shins. "Answer me!"

"Dogh. No. No, no. I don't see any big . . . Glack. Aggg! Blog. Oh my God, my gobg glack!"

"Talk, you Siwash!"

"I don't have nothing to do . . . glack. Agh! Blooooo! Yes. Yes. Yes, yes, yes, yes! He fight. He strong. I do nothing. I knock out. I see nothing. Glob. Blooooo! Ahhhhhhh!"

George Fishcatcher, thought Norton, was probably telling the truth. At least there was no reason to try to get anything more out of him for a while for the way he sprawled on the slimy walk, his moments of consciousness were over.

Norton took a quick run through the Siwash's pockets and found a few messed-up papers. These he appropriated and then dragged George Fishcatcher up the black walk to the first door. He opened this and tossed George inside where George lay emptily on the cheap but gaudy rug.

"What the hell's the idea?" brayed the woman.

Norton threw a ten-dollar bill on top of George Fishcatcher. "Roll him over in the corner and throw a sack on him. If he comes around slip him a Mickey. Okay, sister?"

"Well . . . "

"Okay." Norton closed the door and went back to Stedman Street and Indian Town. Some people were clustered in his way watching a fight between two women in front of the Sunset Liquor Store. He went across the street to the Federal Building side and so on up into respectable Ketchikan. He would not have stopped at the Sourdough but the taxi driver in front hailed him.

"You Mr. Norton?"

"Yes."

"I just took a message in to the clerk for you."

"Who gave it to you?"

"Some Siwash. They all look alike."

"With a split eye?"

"Damned if I know."

Norton went in and got the note:

> If you want to keep healthy go back to Juneau. If you don't you'll be sorry, see? If you do, we'll ship your little pal to you reasonably intact. There is a boat, the *Alaskan*, sailing tonight for Juneau at 12:45 AM. If you aren't on it they'll find your pal the same way they found England.

# CHAPTER FOUR

I N his room Norton found another surprise. Although his door was locked, within all his clothes were packed. Not carefully for here and there a shirt cuff, tie or pants leg protruded from a bag.

Norton picked up the phone. To the clerk he said, "Would you please tell me if Miss Halloway is in the hotel?"

"Yeah. But it won't do you no good, pardner."

"What is her room number?"

"Twenty-six."

"Thanks." Norton put down the phone and stood looking at his packed bags. It was all too evident from past performance that the person who had written that note had ways of carrying out his threat. It was also apparent that Chick was being held for that exact purpose.

The decision was difficult. Should he stick to this track and follow through on the slim clues he had? Even if it meant the life of Chick Star? Or should he take the boat on the chance that it would save Chick's life?

It was now ten minutes to midnight. In fifty-five minutes, unless he went to Juneau, Chick Star would probably be dumped into Tongass Narrows. Maybe Chick was already dead and the promise of return a lie.

Had he been backed up by any forces of law, Norton would

have had the town turned upside down. But forces of law which would actively help him were forty-five hundred miles away, in Washington.

He ran through his pockets and took out of them the papers he had gotten from George Fishcatcher. He already had a definite clue in the name of the boat, the *Roger Halloway*, which would be one of the fleet which Elaine's grandfather had owned and which Elaine now either fought to regain or really controlled.

Odds and ends of bills, cigarette papers and stray scraps made up the contents of Fishcatcher's pockets. Spreading them out on the bureau, Norton found a voucher on the First Territorial Bank made to the credit of George Fishcatcher and drawn on the account of the Halloway Halibut Company for "services during this summer." It was signed in a messy hand which, deciphered, read Tarlof Gregorovna. Russian Tarlof, then, paid the salary of George Fishcatcher, onetime defendant in a dope peddling charge. Russian Tarlof, furthermore, represented the Halloway interests at least for the *Roger Halloway*, one of the fleet.

Another piece of paper caught Norton's interest. It was a pink scrap which bore the printed name of "Montgomery and Roebuck" at the bottom and had smudged penciling on its middle. The piece of paper was identical with that found on James England. But this time it was possible to make out the writing.

"'Love Me Tonight' for Joe and Eddy from Flora."

Norton scowled at the silly message and crammed it in his

pocket. Then for some time he worked about his room. At five after midnight he phoned down to the desk.

"Have my bags put aboard the *Alaskan*. I'll settle my account when I come by the desk."

"You're the boss, pardner."

Norton went out, leaving his door ajar. He went down the hall to twenty-six and knocked. There was no answer. A considerable draft of air seemed to be coming through the crack under the door, making a dismal moaning sound. Norton knocked again. A dull thump-thump greeted his voice.

Norton reached into his pocket and brought out a skeleton key and opened the door. The curtains at the open window blew violently inwards, bringing a few gallons of water with the wind. The door slammed behind Norton.

Elaine Halloway's eyes were frightened and pleading. The gag in her mouth was of wood, pushed in and tied harshly. Her hands were held up by a rope which went over the antique chandelier. A short coil of line was loosely wrapped about her feet, its ends dangling. She seemed to be signaling something with her eyes, darting them toward the window.

Norton stepped to the flying curtains. There was a dripping fire escape just outside and a dark figure was just now swinging off the counterbalanced steel ladder. The man below, a shadow against the rain-polished street, paused after he let the ladder swing back up. He saw Norton. Hugging hard into the building the man raced up to the corner and turned out of sight, disappearing so swiftly that Norton had no time to get at his gun.

Turning to Elaine, Norton did not, for a moment, offer to do anything. He was suspicious of the corners of the room and the bathroom and inspected them. Then he came up beside the girl. The table had been pulled out from the window and pushed within her reach. The hotel pen and ink were on it and a new piece of blotting paper. Norton took the blotting paper over to the mirror and read its first stain:

"Elaine Halloway."

He came back to the girl and untied the gag. He let go the rope at the bed and allowed her to drop her arms. She said nothing but sat where she was trying to rub the circulation back into her wrists.

"Thank you," said Elaine Halloway after a little.

Norton didn't answer her. He was poking into the wastebasket and he pulled out another pink slip of paper with "Montgomery and Roebuck" printed on it.

"'The Devil and the Deep Blue Sea' for Roger from Gertie."

"What's this?" said Norton.

"I never saw it before."

"Then how did it get into your wastebasket?"

"I don't know."

"Who was that who was just in here?"

She shook her head. "I don't know."

"Didn't you get a look at him?"

"Yes, but I had never seen him before."

"What did he want you to sign?"

"I didn't sign anything." She walked controlledly to the mirror and straightened her makeup.

"Look," said Norton, and rubbed the blotter on his shirt

cuff. Some of the ink was still wet enough to stain the white cuff.

"What's the idea of lying to me about everything in sight?" said Norton. "If you come through with the truth it will make it easier when they haul you up before a Federal judge to take a long rap."

She whirled upon him, her face paling, leaving two bright spots of color on her cheekbones, to stand out like bloodstains. "You haven't anything on me!"

"This paper connects you with the death of James England."

"To hell with that piece of paper, G-man. You can't prove my visitor didn't throw it in there!"

"Tell me now that you don't still control the Halloway Halibut Fleet," said Norton.

"I do not and never have. My grandfather left it in charge of Stoddard and when the income fell off I came up here and Hecklin wouldn't turn the papers over to me."

"Where is this Stoddard?"

"I don't know. I've never seen him."

"Or heard from him?"

"He sent me his resignation and said he was going outside. That's all I know."

"Ever hear of one Russian Tarlof Gregorovna?"

She was holding her left arm above the wrist and now she reeled slightly. When she tried to get her balance by gripping the bureau edge, Norton saw that the sleeve of her left arm had been burned. He glanced at the ash tray and saw it was half full of old-fashioned matches.

He stepped to her side and took her hand. Plainly the

intruder had used burning matches against the forearm. Unreasonably Norton was furious. And this contradictory state of affairs made him more angry.

"You're hurt. I'll get something."

"No. Leave me alone. I'm all right. I've been getting along without you splendidly and I guess I can keep on."

He found some cold cream and though she resisted he put a coating of the grease over the deep burns. She had no thanks in her expression. Her full lips curled in disgust.

"If you weren't such a stupid, conceited fool this wouldn't have happened. Why feel sorry about it now?" she demanded.

"Maybe I'm wrong," said Norton. "Maybe you're in a tough spot at that."

"Certainly I am, but I don't want any sympathy from you at this late hour. All you can do is stew around and bully and I've got lots more of that than I can stand. Now get out of here and leave me alone."

"Listen, Miss Halloway, I may have been wrong, but it seemed to me that that attack on you was staged to suck me into a street fight."

"If it was, then does that prove I was in on it?"

"You sat within ten feet of the two men who did it right in the Medlin Hotel Restaurant. When you went out they came over and seemed sore because of the way I had talked to you. Explain that!"

"I never could have seen them before if I didn't recognize them when I was sitting with you that morning."

"Maybe. This slip of pink paper . . ."

"I don't know where it came from."

Norton looked at her. He began to feel desperately sorry for the girl and, at the same time, a little in awe of the way she was bearing up despite the pain which must be in her arm. Maybe he was getting old and cantankerous. Maybe he was in the doldrums because of the weather. Maybe when a man had been in the FBI for six years he got distrustful of everything.

"I'm sorry I didn't give you a break," said Norton.

"Well . . . maybe things did look bad for me."

Norton smiled at her furtively. Down deep he wanted to be friends with this girl, for he admired her now. "Let me go out and find you a doctor and we'll get some good care taken of that arm."

"Oh, no. You'll miss your boat!"

That was a cold icicle in his chest. "And how did you know anything about my boat?"

"The . . . well . . . the man who was in here said you were leaving tonight. And . . . and that I wouldn't have any help from you even if I wanted it now."

"And you are still anxious to see me get aboard?"

"He . . . he said that if you didn't go you'd be killed and . . ." She reddened. "I didn't want to see you killed no matter how you had treated me."

Norton studied her. How neatly she tied these doubts into a string of apparent truth. Did she have such a swift mind that she could cover up blunders and yet be so stupid that she would continue to make blunders?

51

"You doubt me, don't you? I don't blame you much, I guess. A fellow like you always looks at the blackest side of the scales. Must be tough on a temper."

"Leave my temper alone."

"I come up here into a strange world, run into a lot of strange occurrences and situations, find people are anxious to get rid of me and then, to finish me off, discover that my fondest belief is not true. I thought law was always on the side of honest people, that the forces of right and order would rally instantly to the side of the abused, bringing swift justice. Now I find that law is as much at the command of the evildoer as it is under the order of the honest people."

"That is sort of tough on me, isn't it? If I hadn't made the error of supposing at first that there was something definitely wrong about you, or if you had come to me with a complete story I might have saved you from this treatment tonight."

"Forget that part of it. I got what I deserved."

"When you feel better you write me a letter outlining your whole case and I'll do what I can. Make a formal complaint and I'll see that it gets into the hands of proper authority. That's all I can do."

"Then you *are* leaving tonight."

"I can't do much else."

"I . . . I wish we had been better friends."

Norton smiled at her and went to the door. But before his hand touched the knob there was a knock. He opened and saw the clerk standing there.

"This's for you, a feller said," mumbled the clerk at Miss Halloway.

"For me? I'm not expecting anything. There's a mistake."

"I'll take it," said Norton, pulling the package away from the clerk and shutting the door in the fellow's face.

She appeared nervous as she reached for the package.

"Wait," said Norton. "If things are as you say they are then there's a good chance that this thing ticks. Not that anybody up here is that big time but we won't take chances."

She stood back and let him put it into the washbowl in the bathroom and run water on it. When it had soaked for a short while he gingerly pried off the outer wrapper.

"I don't think it is anything explosive," she said.

"You seem nervous about something."

"No. No, I'm not nervous. But after all, that package was sent to me."

"You shouldn't take chances," said Norton.

The outer wrapper fell away in the water and disclosed an odd box. It was made of inch-thick cork. Norton opened it with his penknife. Inside were twelve glass vials, tightly sealed, containing a white and sparkling powder.

Norton broke a seal. He touched his finger in water and then picked up some of the powder on it, smelling it.

He faced Elaine Halloway. "You ought to tell your agents to be more careful. Five hundred dollars worth of heroin shouldn't be allowed to wander into the hands of FBI agents."

She looked wonderingly at the powder and then at Norton. "Heroin?"

"You are accomplished in many ways, fair lady, but you were never cut out to be a clever crook."

"What . . . what are you going to do with me?"

"There's nothing I can do with you just now and you can thank the Fates for that. But you can't get out of Ketchikan for three days and even if you did I could have you picked up in Seattle. You'd better sit here and wait. Now tell me where you've put Chick Star?"

"Who?"

"My young associate."

"I don't even know him."

"You don't know him but you've either murdered him or had him put away somewhere."

"You'll never rest now until you've hung everything on me, including Lincoln's assassination, I suppose."

"I won't risk Star's life and there's nothing I can do. I am going to Juneau tonight. If Star is sent back to me unharmed then I'll make things easier. If he isn't I won't rest until several have floated in his path down Tongass Narrows. That seems to be justice in this country and that's the way I'll have to play the hand. I can't even take a chance on your having him because somebody *did* come in here and force you into signing something. I'll give you that doubt and if Star comes back intact we'll forget about that part of the charge. After that it's every man for himself."

"You're . . . really going to Juneau then?"

"Yes."

"In spite of the awful way things look, I suppose I owe you my thanks and, to be melodramatic about it, my life. He would have killed me afterwards if you hadn't scared him off."

"And you don't know who it was?"

"No."

"Another lie to chalk up," said Norton. He put the heroin into his pocket. "We may meet again, very soon, and when we do the interview won't finish this way."

"I hope not," said Elaine Halloway.

Norton was disdainfully admiring of the way she could act. She had tears in her eyes now. He slammed the door and went down to the desk and paid his bill.

# CHAPTER FIVE

THE SS *Alaskan*'s fifteen-minute whistle blew while Norton was paying his accounts at the desk to a sleepy clerk. Norton went down toward the dock. The steamer was a white decked wall at the end of the street. People were standing around in the rain and others were leaning over the rails bidding interminable goodbyes. Norton went into the steamship office and bought his ticket for Juneau.

At the end of the room two men swathed in yellow oilskins, their faces in the shadow, were elaborately disinterested in what Norton was doing. When Norton got his ticket he looked wryly at them.

"Goodbye, boys," said Norton in a loud voice.

The two looked at him, startled. Momentarily he glimpsed their faces. Here were two halibut fishermen he had not seen before but there were hundreds of their like in Ketchikan. They swiftly looked away.

Norton went out and showed his tickets to the purser at the bottom of the gangway. A steward shuffled up to inquire after Norton's grips. Norton indicated them in the pile of waiting luggage but would not let the steward carry them. The steward scowled blackly upon the practice of a passenger carrying his own bags and wondered without coming to a decision how he could discourage the idea from spreading.

Norton climbed up the gangway to the smeary deck and entered a dark, dirty passageway upon which opened the first-class staterooms. He put his grips down in a cramped cubicle, typical of the Alaskan run of cabins. Two cabin mates were already there, trying to fight the top off a bottle so that their godspeed-bidding friends could have "one lash drink." Norton threw down his grips on an upper bunk and went out. Visitors were being shoved ashore for it was now within two or three minutes of sailing.

Norton went down a ladder and found a passageway which ran the length of the vessel below both well decks. An engineer stared at him.

"Passengers ain't supposed to come down here."

"I'm looking for my dog," said Norton.

"Huh," said the engineer, wandering off.

Norton went forward under the fo'c's'le head. A ladder led up to the deck in the eyes of the ship. Norton thrust his head into the air and looked around. As he had noted before boarding, there was a deep sag in the mooring line here and the cargo lights and dock lights left this place in darkness. As yet no deck hands were standing by to cast off. Norton wrapped his white coat into a bundle under his belt rather than have it give him away.

Norton took a ship's towel, purloined in the cabin, from his pocket and threw it over the hawser. He dropped his weight on both ends of it and, swinging to make it jump, slid downwards from the ship.

As it was close to high tide the water was close to his heels at the center of the line. The towel refused to bite on the upgrade and any instant sailors would come to throw off this line.

A halibut boat was moored with its stern a few feet forward of the *Alaskan*'s bow. Norton started the hawser swinging sideways. Risking a twisted leg, he let go at the forward side of the swing and flew several feet through the air to land on the broad stern of the fishing craft.

He straightened up, having checked his fall by grabbing a gurdy, and cast about for a ladder up to the dock. It was hard to see through the thick rain and dark, and he groped his way forward, searching the pilings with his hand extended. He came up within eight feet of a door without luck. Definitely without luck. The door was flung open from within and a halibut fisherman in yellow oils stood there, stabbing a flashlight at his face. Norton threw up his left hand to fend off the blinding glare. He did not see the meaty hand reach for him. He was yanked forward and, in the same motion, pitched through the door of the deckhouse and down the companionway to the deck of the cabin.

The six-foot fall stunned him for a moment and from far off he heard a harsh voice say, "Eddy! Nail him! I said the son would try it."

"Okay, Joe."

A ton weight dropped on Norton, pinning him down. A fist the size of a twenty-pound load drove straight down at his face.

Norton was conscious enough to roll his head. The halibut

fisherman's fist hit the deck hard enough to crack the planking under the greasy linoleum. Norton used the interval of bawling rage to insert his heels in the fisherman's stomach and straighten them out.

Eddy sailed back against the legs of the descending Joe. Norton sought to get up and draw but his revolver was in his raincoat, which was still wadded up under his belt.

A rack of cleaning knives was close by Joe's huge hand and one of them leaped forth. Joe booted Eddy from underfoot and dived for Norton.

In his backward scramble Norton hit the Mascot coal stove with his hand, burning himself. But with the glitter of that knife he was not interested in minor burns. A kettle of water was boiling in the stove rack. Norton in one motion scooped it by the handle and threw it violently at Joe. Scalding water sprayed about Joe's throat and down inside his oils.

Paying no heed to his howling partner, Eddy began to empty the knife rack, throwing them, hard as he could in this confined space, the whole length of the cabin at Norton.

Norton lifted a kapok cushion from the bunk and, making himself small, scrambled backwards into the forward gear locker where he had a small entrance to defend. He still had no time to get at his gun for a maddened Joe was coming back into the fray, snatching down a thirty-thirty. Evidently the carbine was not loaded for he swung it by the barrel as a club and battered at the protecting cushion, shouting a thunder of words only a halibut fisherman would know. He did not have enough room to properly swing the rifle and backed up, searching madly for a more murderous weapon.

60

At the head of the forepeak bunk was a fire extinguisher of the pump type. Norton snatched it down as a battering weapon and smashed Joe's hand the moment it was laid on the entrance to the gear locker. Joe reeled back, thrusting the broken fingers under his arm and swearing incoherently.

Norton reversed the extinguisher and released its handle. He pumped a forceful stream into Joe's unprotected eyes. The carbon tetrachloride blinded. A lungful of it made Joe stop swearing.

Eddy had not been able to see exactly what had happened, so narrow was the cabin at its forward end. Eddy had found shells for the carbine and thrust its muzzle at Norton. A hard stream caught Eddy in the teeth and then the eyes. The carbine, pointing down, went off, driving a hole through the deck and bottom of the boat. Eddy tore up the bunk with his clawing.

Norton stepped out and smashed the blind and speechless Joe on the button with the fire extinguisher. Joe dropped into Eddy's path and was soundly kicked. Norton bent in the side of the extinguisher on Eddy from behind.

Throwing the extinguisher and the rifle out the open port, Norton went up into the pilothouse. He locked the companionway and then locked the cabin door. He went up the steel ladder to the dock.

From here he saw that the name of the boat was the *Ezra Halloway*. He was sore at himself for having been sucked into such an obvious trap. Evidently somebody was in on this deal who could do some fast thinking and who missed very little.

He stood in the shadows, getting his breath back and ordering his thoughts. Somebody who had been watching the *Alaskan* pull out noticed Norton.

"Fight down there, huh?"

"Yeah," said Norton. "Fight."

"Halibut fisherman," said the loafer and wandered off shaking his head.

The fact that his leaving the *Alaskan* had been anticipated lay heavily in Norton's mind. The statement Joe had made, to wit, "I said the son would try it," directed Norton's thoughts along a different path.

That Elaine Halloway had been forced to sign a paper of some sort, if coupled with the dubiously truthful statement she had made about Hecklin's telling her that he now owned the fleet, rather pointed toward Hecklin. He would have to have evidence of some sort to show, if his ownership—providing that existed or was claimed—of the Halloway fleet was ever questioned. Hence an attempt to wring a signature out of Elaine. There were a lot of loose ends to the idea but Norton, in Chick's interests, thought it best to pursue a course to a swift solution even if he had to leap at wild conclusions.

Norton went up past the fish derricks, past Ketchikan cold storage, and again away from the docks into the town. He had a definite idea of where Hecklin lived—on a hill overlooking Ketchikan. It was an imposing residence visible from the water and locally referred to as "the house in the mist" due to the habit of the fog and rain coming just low enough, at times, to give the place a spectral appearance. The house was close to and about on a level with the top of the radio station's antenna mast.

Norton went along the upper road, crossing Fish Creek above the city's questionable district of Indian Town and passing by the park. It was a constant upgrade. The houses thinned out. An arch at the foot of an upward-vanishing flight of wooden steps was the entrance to the Hecklin home. Norton climbed up, pausing every landing to look ahead and behind, aware of a certain atmosphere in this place. After a considerable climb he saw that the house above was glaringly lighted and heard excited voices emanating from it.

Below, brakes yelped and two doors slammed. Several footbeats made the long stairway shake. Norton sped on ahead and dived off into the bushes at a landing in time to let Chief of Police Danton, Kelly and a doctor leap upward and by.

Amazed, Norton swiftly but unobtrusively followed in their wake. The trio were quickly let into the home. Norton saw that the hill was too steep around the place to get from the front to the rear and so took the only course left. He let the heavy knocker fall.

A dazed Filipino let him in. A cook stood in the door of a far room winding her apron around her hands. A woman, possibly Mrs. Hecklin, sat in the study, eyes hidden by her moist handkerchief.

Norton walked through past the cook.

Hecklin was lying on a blood spattered bed, his evil old face the color of a dead salmon, his hands clenching at the spread.

The doctor pulled open the dressing gown at the chest and ripped away the shirt. Hecklin was a rather gory mess. There was a round hole in the center of his chest which was pumping blood.

"Is he in bad shape?" said Chief Danton, helping himself to a box of cigars on the desk by the bed.

"Don't know yet," said the doctor. "Small caliber bullet. Seems to have punctured a lung. Why the hell don't you get somebody to tell you how it happened and leave my end of it alone."

"Well, if he's dead, then that's murder. And if he isn't dead then that's just mayhem."

"This is Hecklin," said the doctor.

That fact seemed to come home to Chief Danton and Kelly. They went out and collared the Filipino.

"How did this happen?" said Danton to the shaking brown boy.

"I don't know. I hear a shot and come to room. I come in and Mister Hecklin lying on floor. Window open. Is he dead?"

"How do we know you didn't do it?" said Danton to the brown boy.

"I heard the shot too," said the white woman in the study. "Enrico wasn't even near. The door was locked from the inside and Enrico had to break it open with an axe."

"Where was the cook?" said Kelly.

"I vas in da kitchen, you sneaking Irish," said the big cook with a defiant nod of her head. "You leave Enrico alone or I take a cleaver to you."

"Dead end," said Chief Danton. "Now, Mrs. Hecklin, we

hate to bother you with questions, but did you see anybody come in the house earlier this evening?"

"No one," said Mrs. Hecklin. "Thomas was in his room going to bed."

"Well, we'll have a look in there," said Kelly. He walked into the bedroom again and ran into Norton who was helping the doctor get Hecklin straightened out. "Huh!" said Kelly. "Where did you come from?"

"I just arrived," said Norton.

"You run along," said Danton. "We'll attend to this."

Norton, having helped the doctor all he could, stood back, waiting for a further excuse to linger. Hecklin's safe was open and papers were strewn around in front of it. Lying hard by the laboring doctor's feet was a patent leather pocketbook, black with a large brass buckle.

"Small caliber bullet," announced the doctor, producing it.

Norton took it out of his fingers and though Kelly yanked it away almost as soon as he touched it, Norton could see that it was a .25.

"If he dies," said Danton, "somebody will hang for this. Maybe."

"Looks like self-defense to me," said Norton.

"Huh? Self-defense for who?"

"For the person who shot Hecklin. See that?"

Partially hidden by a fold of the sheet was a Colt Frontiersman. Danton scooped it up eagerly and inspected it.

"Probably has Hecklin's initials on it," said Norton.

Danton turned it around and around. "I don't see anything on it." He threw it down, having obliterated any fingerprints

65

on it, particularly Norton's who had scooped it out of a drawer and thrown it on the bed while the doctor was trying to separate cotton packs.

"The killer evidently went out that window," suggested Norton.

Kelly went over and leaned on the sill and then bent far out, his dripping raincoat getting the entire sill wet.

"You'd have to go outside to see where he went," said Norton.

Kelly did not like to follow the suggestion but it was too obviously the correct procedure, so far as he could see, to be ignored. Kelly lifted himself through the window and dropped heavily on the side of the hill, starting a small avalanche. He poked a flashlight at the ground.

"Hell," said Danton, from the window, "you went and stamped out the footprints."

Norton swung the handle of the safe back and forth a time or two and pulled open a few inner compartments.

"Let that alone," growled Danton. "Say! You'll wipe out the fingerprints."

"Sorry," said Norton, standing up.

"Clumsy," reproved Danton. "I thought you guys were supposed to know about such things."

"We'll have to get him to the hospital," said the doctor. "Send for an ambulance. He'll live, I think, but he may have to have a transfusion."

Danton called for an ambulance and, a little later, the intern and his driver were struggling down the long slippery steps, bearing Hecklin on a stretcher.

Norton went into the kitchen. "Are you sure you didn't hear anything?"

The cook shook her head. "Yust a shot."

"I suppose Hecklin had a lot of enemies," said Norton.

"No. Course that is pretty hort to say. He vas a hort man, Mister Hecklin."

Norton kept it up until he was sure the police weren't coming back. He went into the bedroom where Hecklin had been shot and swiftly hauled the pocketbook from where he had kicked it—under the bureau. He put it inside his coat and went out.

"I'm sure your husband will be all right," he said to Mrs. Hecklin.

"Oh, I hope so. He has been so worried lately that his health has been very poor."

"Good night," said Norton.

He went down the steps to the street and made his way across into the darkness of the other side. Under cover of a bush he inspected the pocketbook. As he had supposed it contained letters to Elaine Halloway, a compact initialed E. H. and an identification card.

He was not quite sure why he had covered her up so thoroughly, staging a self-defense angle in case the police ever caught up to her, getting her prints wiped off the sill and safe if her prints had been on them. He had the solace of knowing he had not interfered too much with the case. In an inside pocket, carefully wrapped in a linen handkerchief, he had the assault weapon which he had taken from under the bathrobe of Thomas Hecklin. Hecklin had evidently sought to save himself by clutching the weapon. He had not avoided the shot but he had at least retained, unbeknownst to himself, a full set of fingerprints of the attacker. Kelly had the slug from the gun. Norton had the gun and the fingerprints. Well, Kelly wouldn't have known what to have done with them anyway.

# CHAPTER SIX

ELAINE HALLOWAY came up the steps to the second floor of the Sourdough Hotel. Her face was tense with concern as she glanced up and down the dim corridor. Quickly she inserted a key in her lock and opened the door. Her hand went out to the switch and the lights went on.

She stumbled back with a gasp. Norton reached out and slammed the door shut behind her. He put out his hands to help her out of the rain cape and she turned to let him remove it. He hung it on a chair where it could drip.

"Late to be running around Ketchikan," said Norton.

"I . . . I had to find a drugstore and get something for my arm."

"And you have it with you, I suppose?"

"No. I . . . Oh!" She had spotted her pocketbook lying on the bed and snatched it up. "Where did you find it? It had all my money in it and I was so upset that I forgot to take it with me. I couldn't pay the clerk and said I'd have to come back for some money first."

"What a mind," said Norton, not without admiration.

"What do you mean? Where did you find my purse?"

"Where you left it."

"Right here?"

"No."

She looked into the purse again and missed something. "What have you done with my automatic?"

"It is in a safe place," said Norton, touching his raincoat over his chest.

"Why did you take it?" said Elaine.

"To save your pretty neck, my lady."

"Oh. I still don't understand. I've carried it since I was attacked that night. I wouldn't use it unless I had to."

"Naturally Hecklin forced you to use it."

"Hecklin? What does he have to do with this?"

"Listen, Miss Halloway, I am interested in three things. The disappearance of Jerry McCain, special agent, the presence of heroin in Ketchikan and its import into the States from here, and the whereabouts and health of Chick Star. I am not interested, particularly, in the shooting of Hecklin tonight."

"Hecklin? Shot? By whom?"

"Lady, must you always pretend? I have here the weapon. It is your gun. It was left on the scene in Hecklin's hand. Your purse was also there. You went to Hecklin to get back that paper he made you sign and when he protested you shot him and got it anyway. That was pretty coldblooded and even in Alaska murder is sometimes punished. Hecklin is dying in the local hospital."

"You mean . . . you think . . . I shot Hecklin?"

"You seem to be the only one carrying your own purse."

"You got my purse and gun at Hecklin's house?"

"Where you left them."

"But you're mad! It wasn't Hecklin who was here tonight."

"Then who was it?"

"I don't know!"

"We won't quibble about this," said Norton. "As I said before I am interested in three things. Jerry, dope and Chick Star. Right now it is Chick Star. Tonight I persuaded one George Fishcatcher to tell me that he was off the *Roger Halloway*. You know George Fishcatcher."

"Do I?"

"He is an Indian in your employ."

"I employ no one. I tell you I have nothing to do with my fleet. I know nothing about either dope or your friend."

"I saw you stop and talk to George Fishcatcher outside the Federal Building."

"Oh. That Indian. He said he was a friend of my grandfather's and that if I needed help to let him know. I told him I needed no help."

"What a plausible person you are," said Norton. "But we won't argue. Chick Star may be aboard one of your boats, perhaps the *Roger Halloway* which, I think, is skippered by Russian Tarlof. If I went down there by myself they would probably shoot me on sight. Now we'll make a deal. I will forget what you did to Hecklin if you will lead me to Chick Star and confess to the dope rap. Hecklin dead means your execution. I am the only one who knows you did it. A dope rap will mean, at most, twenty years, twelve on good behavior, and you will still be a young woman when you come out."

She was tall in her anger. "Mr. Norton, you have gone too far. You threaten me with the chair and then with prison. For what? I have done nothing!"

"Quit the dramatics," said Norton. "If you will go down to

the *Roger Halloway* and get yourself aboard, thus distracting attention so that I can get the gentlemen covered, I will forget about this murder."

"No."

"Then," said Norton, getting up, "I will have to go to Chief Danton and tell him where he can find the murderer of Thomas Hecklin and give him the proof."

"Go ahead and tell him. Go ahead and make more trouble for me, who already has enough to last eight lifetimes. If you had come to me and asked me to do this for you without all this threatening and bullying I would have helped you all I could but now, sir, you can go straight to hell!"

Norton paused at the door. He could not but admire the majesty of her. "If I asked you nicely right now, would you help me?"

"What would I get out of it?"

"So you can drive bargains too," said Norton.

"Why not?"

"And what do you want out of it?"

"That any charge against the Halloway Fleet for running heroin be dropped. You can arrest whoever you wish but you cannot confiscate the boats."

Norton stared. "I must say that you can ask enough."

"Only under those conditions will I aid you to get your friend back."

Norton was angry now. "All charges against the boats dropped and no confiscation of them?"

"Yes."

"But I can arrest whoever I please?"

"Yes."

"Including yourself?"

"If you can find any real evidence against me. Yes."

"Huh. All right. I know when I'm bested. Put on your cape and we'll go to the *Roger Halloway*. You're very confident of having covered yourself up in this matter."

"Why not be? I have nothing to fear."

"You don't know the meaning of the word, you blonde fool."

She let it pass and put on her cape. Norton led the way out of the room but insisted that she precede him down the steps and across the lobby into the street.

"If you make any signals to anyone," said Norton, "much as I hate to do it, you get shot first." And his hand tightened about the butt of his service .45 in his raincoat pocket. "Lead on."

She knew where she was going. She went up Water Street toward the city floats. The rain had increased in velocity and quantity, its gusts blotting out the lights along this deserted way for a second or two at a time. Ahead and to their left lay a number of fishing boats, trolling poles and decks shining under the swinging dock lights, vanishing and reappearing like some spectral fleet. Elaine Halloway went down the ramp, ducking her head against the torrents of water. With certainty she picked her way up the slippery planks which were rendered only slightly less treacherous by laid chicken wire.

A nest of boats lay on both sides. A swinging light picked out the name *Roger Halloway* on a tall bow. The halibut boat was third out from the float, necessitating their climbing over two boats to get to it. At the gunwale of the first Norton stopped her by touching her arm and discovered that she was shivering.

*Elaine Halloway went down the ramp, ducking her head against the torrents of water. With certainty she picked her way up the slippery planks which were rendered only slightly less treacherous by laid chicken wire.*

"You go to the companionway and sing out for Russian Tarlof," said Norton. "You ask him to come on deck. If he won't and asks that you come below, don't make him suspicious but go below. Remember that there are ports open there and that I will be on the next boat, at one of those ports. When you go below, if you must go below, I will be at that port. When I cover those in the cabin, you pick up any guns and throw them out the other port. If you try to shoot me or in any way hinder me from taking these men, you get my first bullet."

"Pleasant fellow," said Elaine Halloway.

"If Russian Tarlof will come up it will be easier but I don't think he will. Be on your way."

She drew a deep breath and stepped over the gunwale, crossing the first boat. She stepped to the second and crossed its deck. Norton was beside her. He indicated the open port in the hull of the *Roger Halloway* which he could command by standing on the deck of the second boat.

Elaine boarded the *Roger Halloway*. She rapped sharply on the pilothouse door.

Quick movements sounded in the cabin below. Norton was ready to move up and slug Tarlof if he came out.

"Who is there?" rumbled Russian Tarlof.

"Elaine Halloway to see you," said the girl.

There was a thump as the inner hatch went open. The cabin door swung outward. "Who?"

"Elaine Halloway."

"Oh! Huh! What you want?"

"Come on deck for a moment."

"It is too vet. Come below."

Elaine glanced at Norton who had swiftly taken his post beside the port. She stepped into the pilothouse and below.

Norton saw her legs on the hatch ladder and then all of her as she swung down into the cabin. He cast a swift look at the three men in the room. Russian Tarlof still had his arm in a sling but his comrade in that fatal battle was not bearing any signs of it now, outside of a plaster on his broken nose. The third man in the room was a Siwash with a sullen, nearly black face. Russian Tarlof stood back so that Elaine could sit down on the transom by the table.

"Well?" said Russian Tarlof. "I suppose you come to see about things. You got nerve to come down here but I always say blondes have nerve. What can we do for you tonight?"

The Siwash on the bunk and the white man on the other bunk looked quietly but fixedly at Elaine. There was a rifle above the Siwash. Russian Tarlof was only half in Norton's view. Norton had to take his chance for at last resort he could blast them as they tried to come out of the ship.

Norton put his face to the port. "Stand still, gentlemen. I can shoot before you can."

The three whipped about to face him. The Siwash shrank back from the muzzle of the .45 just inside the port. Tarlof's white friend froze to his blankets.

"So!" yelled Tarlof. "You turn squealer! This is a trap!" And while he spoke he moved more quickly than Norton had thought he could. Tarlof, battle-wise, placed himself in front of Elaine so that any bullet going through him might hit her. In the same movement and instant he smashed down the lantern and, by its last glow, threw Elaine off the transom and in front of him, the while diving back out of coverage from the port.

"You she-witch!" bawled Tarlof in the dark.

Elaine screamed. "Norton! He'll . . . kill me!"

Norton called himself a blundering fool. A gigantic doubt surged into his mind and with it mad recriminations. He stabbed his pen-flashlight into the room at risk to himself. The rifle by the Siwash was in instant use, the bullet throwing splinters into Norton's eyes.

Blinded, Norton sought to fumble his way back to get away from the side of the boat. His foot contacted a rope which rolled. He sagged against a stay. The delay detained him too long to permit his reaching the float. He felt about and crouched in the cover of the second boat's pilothouse. Another shot glanced off brass by his head and went yowling away. He crouched lower, trying to clear his sight. He could see vague blurs of lights. He got out a handkerchief and dabbed at his eyes. He had a sick feeling of helplessness. When he took the handkerchief away, though in considerable pain, he could see again. The splinters had gashed his eyelids, filling his sight with blood.

The door of the *Roger Halloway* was flung open and, running low, the Siwash got into cover at the stern of the boat Norton was on. On the starboard side of the *Roger Halloway* a hatch slammed open and the ship heeled away from Norton.

77

The plan was simple and deadly. The Siwash would come up on one side of the house, forcing Norton around until he got his back to Tarlof on the far side of the *Roger Halloway,* in the cover of the pilothouse.

Norton again wiped his eyes. He had missed his chance of getting the Siwash when he had dived from boat to boat. But now he thought he might be able to reverse the obvious and get aboard the boat next to the dock before the Siwash was set. Norton sprang across the gap. The carbine flamed and the slug yanked at Norton's collar. Norton dived to the dock on the far side and quickly went aft along the first boat, covered by the height of its hull. He could not escape up the ramp even had he wanted to—and he did not want to.

For he knew, definitely now, that Elaine Halloway had nothing to do with the activities of Russian Tarlof. Her bargain with Norton had been honest. She had feared to lose her fleet because it had been used in the dope traffic—halibut boats being able to come and go repeatedly in both Canadian and American ports without too much check and able to contact vessels in the Gulf of Alaska, out of sight of land, thus picking up contraband. The Siwash had never seen her before, judging by his expression. And last and most, Elaine Halloway had not shot Hecklin.

Russian Tarlof had mud on his boots. No fisherman had any place to go where he could get fresh sod. On these gravel streets and boardwalks, out on the muskeg, no such mud could be found. But there was mud in the terraced flower garden of the Hecklin home. Red mud, the same color as that which Kelly had had on his boots when he had come back through the window.

Norton understood the enormity of his own crime, sending Elaine Halloway into the hands of these devils, for she would never be let ashore now and if anything happened that Norton could not release her shortly, she would be dead.

Norton saw the silhouette of the Siwash for an instant and fired. The man yowled and scrambled back. The second boat rocked violently and then the first. Russian Tarlof was coming over to cut Norton off from the ramp, himself covered by the pilothouses.

Swiftly Norton leaped up on the stern of the first boat. He saw Russian Tarlof leap from one to the next and fired. But his sight and the rain made him miss.

The third man got into action, firing at Norton from the deck of the *Roger Halloway*. Norton hunched down. That fool over there did not realize that he showed up against the dock lights. Norton aimed carefully and fired. The man straightened up and, stiff-legged, dropped backwards into the water.

Norton worked his way toward the halibut boat. He did not know where the Siwash was or even if the man was badly wounded or not. He did not know where Russian Tarlof was. Crawling down on the decks of the two inner ships he got to the gunwale of the *Roger Halloway*. There was, as yet, no sign of the Siwash.

Hammering came from inside the halibut boat. The inner companionway had been slammed and locked against Elaine's escape.

*Norton saw the silhouette of the Siwash for an instant and fired. The man yowled and scrambled back.*

The fishermen on neighboring boats made no appearance, respecting stray slugs. The rain increased its volume.

Flame flared forward on the *Roger Halloway*. Another shot came from the dock where Russian Tarlof now crouched.

Norton screamed. A coil of hawser on his right had received the slugs. He thrust the coil through the rail and into the water where it splashed loudly.

There was silence then, save for the downpour. Norton crawled as gently as he could from the gunwale aboard the *Roger Halloway*, aft past the fish hatch to the starboard side.

"See anything?" said Tarlof somewhere.

"Not a thing," called back the Siwash.

Norton slid into the open pilothouse and across the deck beneath the wheel. There was no pounding now on the inner hatch. He drew the pin out of the hasp and silently opened it.

"It's Norton," he whispered.

A small gasp of relief came from the darkness of the cabin below.

"Come up here," whispered Norton.

She crawled up through the hatch and he led her slowly back until she was in the engine room. Stray beams of rain-filtered dock light reached through the open door and fell on the cabin companionway. Norton replaced the hasp and pin without a sound. He crawled backwards until he was in the engine room hatch, hidden save for his head. Norton wiped the blood out of his eyes and then replaced the exploded shells in his revolver.

For a long time there was no sound from the dock. Then the *Roger Halloway* listed under a weight.

"See anything?" said the Siwash nervously.

"Nothing, whatever," said Russian Tarlof. "He must have sank."

"I need a drink," said the Siwash. "He got Wrangell."

"We'll squawk about this to the police," said Russian Tarlof.

"I need a drink," shivered the Siwash.

They came into the pilothouse. The Siwash stood with his carbine in the crook of his arm, its muzzle pointing unwittingly at Norton. That was too long a chance.

Norton quietly raised his revolver. Russian Tarlof was opening the hatch.

"Try anything funny down there and I'll smash your brains out!" said Tarlof. "Light the lights below, just to make sure she didn't dig up a gun," he added to the Siwash.

Norton fired.

The bullet took the Siwash between the eyes and slammed him against the wheel, dead before he hit.

Tarlof's reaction carried him out through the port door and down. Norton got a bad shot. Tarlof, seeing he could not make it, lunged back at the flame of the gun. He got the muzzle in hand. Norton fired and the shot took Tarlof in the shoulder. Tarlof wrestled the gun out of Norton's grasp.

Lunging up into his quarry, Norton carried Tarlof backwards. They fell together into the cabin and rolled through the darkness. Tarlof thrust an iron finger into Norton's throat, making Norton writhe in agony.

Somewhere there was a furious hammering but Norton had no attention for that. Tarlof, kicking Norton in the stomach, got free. Norton was in the black cabin with a slightly wounded bear, unarmed, only half-conscious.

There was a rattle and then a crash as the bottom was broken off a bottle. Tarlof had himself a mangling weapon. There was fumbling as Tarlof groped for his victim.

Abruptly a forward compartment door caved in. Someone else was in the midship cabin. Norton heard a snarl as Tarlof gripped another, then violent fighting.

Norton hitched himself up on the sink and found a box of matches. He struck one and located a light switch. The battery lights glared down into the room.

Chick Star, dirty and ragged, still trailing the ends of the ropes which had bound him, was sitting on top of Russian Tarlof slugging him ceaselessly in the face. After a while it became apparent even to Chick that Russian Tarlof had been out for some time.

Chick got up and stepped on Tarlof's stomach. "Why didn't you wait for me?" complained Chick. "I been hours at it but I could have busted loose and nailed these birds when you came into the cabin the first time!"

"I didn't know you were here," said the battered Norton.

"Gosh," said Chick, realizing it was over. "Wasn't this a swell fight. I wish I'd been in on it. Y'know, they threw me in a skiff and rowed me down here. They'd never have taken me but they asked me for a match and as soon as I had a hand in my pocket they saw who it was and slugged me."

Elaine Halloway was kneeling beside Norton, wiping the blood out of his eyes.

"I'm sorry about all that," said Norton. "I've been a fool."

"So have I," said Elaine. "But I was so scared the government would take my boats because of what had been done with them."

"What's going on down there?" said a hard voice, and Kelly dropped down into the cabin. He was rendered speechless by the sight of the place and the dangling leg of the Siwash into which he had bumped.

Chief Danton came below. "Who's been shootin'—" He saw Norton. "You again."

"Me again," said Norton, finding enough energy to stand up.

"What's it about?" said Danton.

Norton paid little heed. He took the prints of Tarlof and then took out the .25 automatic. Even flour showed that Tarlof had shot Hecklin.

Norton reached over and wiped some of the stain off Tarlof's face. Then he called for water and sloshed it on Tarlof until he came groggily around.

"Wake up, England," said Norton.

"What did you call him?" said Danton.

"England," said Norton. "You see, that corpse you pulled out of the narrows was not England."

"How do you know?" challenged Danton.

"Because England, as a radioman, had his prints on file with the FCC. I took prints with a cigarette case of the corpse you found. In the letters I received this afternoon they were stated not to be England's. They belonged to Jerry McCain."

"Say," said Kelly, peering hard at Tarlof. "You do look something like England."

"You are crazy," said Tarlof. "I can prove—"

"You vanished for a month and grew a black beard," said Norton. "You see, England, this print I just took answers to that description of England's which I today received. You killed McCain, got scared, pretended to kill yourself instead."

"That proves nothing!" cried Tarlof.

"These pink slips of paper prove plenty," said Norton. "They are part of the 'Montgomery and Roebuck' request program. By broadcasting certain requests you regulated the activities of the fleet. You made Hecklin an unwilling partner and, when you thought he'd talk, you sought to kill him. You didn't. You've tried to hang the dope running and that attempted murder on Miss Halloway. And this paper which I took from the safe at Hecklin's shows that you made Miss Halloway sign a letter you had written to Hecklin as though from her about her profits in the dope running. You planned very well, England."

"I'm innocent. I, Russian Tarlof—"

"Shall I give him some more?" said Chick Star eagerly.

"He doesn't need any more. Besides, Hecklin told me the whole story earlier this evening."

"He did not!" yelled Tarlof.

"He did. He said you were the head."

"He had a lot to do with it too. He didn't know what was happening with these boats maybe but he had the idea of stealing them and running Stoddard out. You can't hang all this on me. Hecklin is just as guilty—"

"And everything you say will be used against you, England."

"Gosh, he talks like England when he doesn't pull that

phony accent," said Danton. "Say, Norton, you sure know your fingerprints."

Norton did not bother to say that he had yet to hear from Washington about the prints. That his case was a guess. He was tired of the *Roger Halloway*.

Elaine and Chick helped him out of the hatch and to the dock. The rain had let up quite a bit.

Norton looked at Elaine.

# STORY PREVIEW

# STORY PREVIEW

NOW that you've just ventured through one of the captivating tales in the Stories from the Golden Age collection by L. Ron Hubbard, turn the page and enjoy a preview of *Dead Men Kill*. Join Detective-Sergeant Terry Lane as he investigates dual murders and discovers that the killers are already dead! Clue by clue, Lane unveils a plot involving Haitian voodoo and stumbles down a twisted trail towards the evil Dr. Leroux—and a possible fate worse than death.

# DEAD MEN KILL

IN a voice which held the icy tones of death, the dark-clothed man in the open doorway rasped, "I have come to kill you, Gordon! *I have come to kill you!*"

Gordon stiffened in his massive chair. His ruddy face went ashen; his thick fingers clutched at the corners of his desk. "Jackson!" he shrieked.

The killer's eyes were glassy. His hands reached out before him, grasping, talonlike. The pallor of the dead was on his wasted face. He was clothed in the garments of the grave! Silently, relentlessly, he walked forward.

"Stop!" screamed Gordon. "My God, Jackson, what have I ever done to you?"

The answer was toneless, harsh. "I have come to kill you, Gordon!"

The clutching hands came closer. Gordon covered his face, tried to cower away. Beside him was a telephone. Furtively he reached out for it.

If Jackson saw, he gave no heed. Blindly he came against the outer edge of the desk. Slowly he skirted the obstruction and came on.

"Police!" cried Gordon into the receiver.

If Jackson heard, he gave no sign. His hard, glassy eyes,

sunken and horrible, were fixed on his victim's throat. Gordon stared up and caught the odor which had assailed him from the first. It was the smell of moist earth mingled with the perfumes of the undertaking parlor. The stench of the grave!

"I have come to kill you, Gordon!" repeated the murderer. It was as though this phrase was all that remained in the man's mind.

"My God, Jackson! Get away!" Too late, Gordon tried to scramble out from behind his desk.

Jackson lunged, hands convulsing. When the sunken eyes were a foot away from Gordon's, the fingers snapped down on the victim's throat. There was a shriek and the crash of the overturned chair. Gordon whipped about, writhing under the maniacal strength of the hands.

Shuddering sobs were coming from the victim's distorted mouth. Slowly the body under the hands relaxed and lay still. Jackson's fingers still clutched the throat.

Seconds ticked by before the murderer moved. Then, with his expressionless face turned toward the door, he walked slowly from the room.

The toneless phrase came again. "I have come to kill you, Gordon!" And the man who was dressed for the grave disappeared into the corridor.

Inspector Leonard rushed from his desk into the squad room and spotted Detective-Sergeant Terry Lane. "Lane! Snap into it. Gordon's been murdered and I think it's a clue on your Burnham killing. The man on the switchboard heard

Gordon shout 'My God, Jackson, get away!' into the phone. Get out there right away!"

Detective-Sergeant Terrence Lane needed no further word. Like a shot, his wiry figure hurtled through the door, plunged down a flight of steps and swung aboard the scout car at the curb.

"The Gordon residence!" shouted Lane to Monahan at the wheel. "And step on it!"

The car roared up the street, Lane hanging to the running board, his blue eyes flashing, the wind tearing at his raven black hair. Monahan had given the wild figure a brief glance, decided that Terry Lane meant what he said, and the squad car ripped past a red light, lanced up a traffic-jammed avenue, screamed around a curve and then came to a stop before the imposing mansion which was the home of the late Ralph Gordon, a well-known wealthy sportsman.

If Detective Lane was disheveled, he had good reason to be. For a week he had been on the trail of a killer he could never reasonably expect to apprehend. The papers were blatant in their denouncement of the police force in general and Terry Lane in particular.

Since that fatal day seven days before when Edward Burnham, head of a power trust, had been found dead in his home, Lane's life had been a nightmare. He had not known which way to turn, since the only conceivable clue had pointed the guilt to Hamilton, secretary to Burnham. And that was impossible. For Hamilton had been dead and buried for two weeks!

Lane sprinted up the steps, kicked open the front door

and stepped inside. Then, undecided, he stopped and stared about him. In the hall of that great home, in spite of the clamor of traffic outside its door, silence reigned. It was the sinister, clammy silence of death. An odor came to him oppressively.

Worry flicked across Lane's lean, nervous face and he looked down at his feet. There, in the center of the hallway, lay a blue gray cotton glove. When he picked it up, Lane again smelled that faint odor. Suddenly he recognized it.

It was a pallbearer's glove that he had found and from it came the stench of moist earth and sickening perfume. The odor of the grave!

Jamming his first clue into his pocket, Lane ran into the room at his right and then stopped abruptly.

As many times as the detective had witnessed death, his stomach retched at the sight before him. Gordon was sprawled on the floor, rigid and staring. His once-dapper clothes were ripped about the throat. The flesh beneath his jaw was blue and swollen. But it was the face which held Lane's gaze. Surprise, horror and disbelief were mirrored there so strongly that even death had not erased them.

Lane stepped forward with a shudder. He looked quickly about for some telltale bit of evidence, but nothing untoward rewarded him.

From the street came the noise of sirens and screeching brakes, heralding the arrival of the wagon and the coroner. With them, Lane knew, would come the newshawks and cameramen. He dreaded their arrival more than he did the prospects of solving this second murder. It was certain that a few more scathing articles such as those which had recently appeared would ruin Terry Lane's promising career.

To find out more about *Dead Men Kill* and how you can obtain your copy, go to www.goldenagestories.com.

# GLOSSARY

# GLOSSARY

STORIES FROM THE GOLDEN AGE *reflect the words and expressions used in the 1930s and 1940s, adding unique flavor and authenticity to the tales. While a character's speech may often reflect regional origins, it also can convey attitudes common in the day. So that readers can better grasp such cultural and historical terms, uncommon words or expressions of the era, the following glossary has been provided.*

---

**blackjack:** a short, leather-covered club, consisting of a heavy head on a flexible handle, used as a weapon.

**button, on the:** a blow on the tip of the chin; jawbreaker; a hard blow that usually causes a knockout.

**carbine:** a short light rifle.

**chee-chalker:** a newcomer to Alaska and the Klondike; an Indian word meaning one who is inexperienced or has no knowledge; a tenderfoot.

**Colt Frontiersman:** Colt Frontier Six-Shooter; a .44-caliber, single-action revolver made by the Colt Firearms Company, established in 1847 by Samuel Colt (1814–1862). The Colt Frontier was originally made to be compatible with

.44-caliber "Winchester Central Fire" cartridges, a cartridge that was commonly used in Winchester rifles.

**Colt revolver:** Colt Detective Special; a short-barreled revolver first produced in 1927 by the Colt Firearms Company. Though originally offered as a .32 caliber, the most common of the Colt Detective Specials were .38 caliber and had a two-inch barrel. The short barrel design made this gun popular for use as a concealed weapon by plainclothes police detectives.

**eyes of the ship:** the forwardmost portion of the topmost deck of a ship, as far forward as a person can stand. The name comes from the ancient Chinese custom of painting eyes on each bow so that the ship could see where she was going.

**Fates:** the Fates, in classical mythology, are the three goddesses Clotho, Lachesis and Atropos, who control human destiny.

**fo'c's'le head:** forecastle head; the part of the upper deck of a ship at the front. The forecastle is the front of a ship, from the name of the raised castlelike deck on some early sailing vessels, built to overlook and control the enemy's deck.

**forepeak:** the interior part of a boat or ship nearest the bow.

**forty-five or .45:** a handgun chambered to fire a .45-caliber cartridge.

**fulminate of mercury:** a gray crystalline powder that when dry explodes under percussion or heat and is used in detonators and as a high explosive.

**fusel oil:** an acrid oily liquid occurring in insufficiently distilled alcoholic liquors. Used especially as a source of alcohols and as a solvent.

**gangway:** a narrow, movable platform or ramp forming a bridge by which to board or leave a ship.

**gibbet:** an upright post with a crosspiece, forming a T-shaped structure from which criminals were formerly hanged for public viewing.

**G-men:** government men; agents of the Federal Bureau of Investigation.

**gunwale:** the upper edge of the side of a boat. Originally a gunwale was a platform where guns were mounted, and was designed to accommodate the additional stresses imposed by the artillery being used.

**gurdy:** a reel with a crank used to pull in fishing nets on a boat.

**hard by:** in close proximity to; near.

**hawser:** a thick rope or cable for mooring or towing a ship.

**Juneau:** port city in southeastern Alaska. In 1900 it was made the capital of the territory of Alaska and later the state capital when Alaska joined the Union in 1959. It is named after the gold prospector Joseph Juneau, who discovered gold in the area in 1880.

**kapok:** a silky fiber obtained from the fruit of the silk-cotton tree and used for insulation and as padding in pillows, mattresses and life preservers.

**Ketchikan:** a city located on the southwestern coast of Revillagigedo Island near the southern boundary of Alaska, and named after the Ketchikan Creek that flows through the town. Much of the town sits over water, supported by pilings. Ketchikan has the heaviest average rainfall in North America and is one of the four wettest spots on Earth. With 160 inches of rain a year, the rainfall is measured in feet, not inches. The locals refer to rain as "liquid sunshine."

**klootches:** Indian women of northwestern Alaska.

**Marquis of Queensberry:** referring to the official rules for the sport of boxing; originated by John Sholto Douglas (1844–1900), a British nobleman and eighth Marquis of Queensberry (a hill in lower Scotland).

**Mascot:** Mascot Stove Company; company that made coal stoves.

**Mickey:** Mickey Finn; a drug-laced drink given to someone without their knowledge in order to incapacitate them. Named after a bartender who, before his days as a saloon proprietor, was known as a pickpocket and thief who often preyed on drunken bar patrons.

**MP:** Military Police.

**muskeg:** a swamp or bog formed by an accumulation of moss, leaves and decayed matter resembling peat.

**newshawk:** a newspaper reporter, especially one who is energetic and aggressive.

**physiognomy:** the features of somebody's face, especially when they are used as indicators of that person's character or temperament.

**rotgut:** raw, inferior liquor.

**sap:** blackjack; a short, leather-covered club, consisting of a heavy head on a flexible handle, used as a weapon.

**Scheherazade:** the female narrator of *The Arabian Nights,* who during one thousand and one adventurous nights saved her life by entertaining her husband, the king, with stories.

**scow:** an old or clumsy boat; hulk; tub.

**seine boat:** fishing boat; a boat specially constructed to carry and utilize a seine, a large net. One edge of the net is provided with sinkers and the other with floats. It hangs vertically in the water and when its ends are brought together or drawn ashore it encloses the fish.

**Sitka:** a port city in the southern part of Alaska, on the Pacific Ocean.

**Siwash:** a North American Indian of the Pacific Northwest, Northwest Canada and Alaska.

**"snow":** cocaine or heroin in the form of a white powder.

**sou'wester:** a waterproof hat with a wide brim that widens in the back to protect the neck in stormy weather, worn especially by seamen.

**SS:** steamship.

**stern:** the rear end of a ship or boat.

**thirty-eight:** thirty-eighth parallel north; an imaginary circle of latitude that is thirty-eight degrees north of the Earth's equator. The thirty-eighth parallel north runs through the United States of America.

**thirty-thirty** or **.30-30:** Winchester model 1894 rifle that is chambered to fire a .30-30 cartridge, the first North American sporting cartridge designed for use with smokeless powder. The .30-30 is a .30-caliber cartridge that was originally loaded with 30 grains of the new smokeless powder, which is the source of its name.

**Thomas Basin:** a boat harbor in Ketchikan, Alaska.

**Tlingits:** a Native American people inhabiting the coastal and island areas of southeast Alaska.

**Tongass Narrows:** the channel of water that runs between Ketchikan and Gravina Island, located in the southern part of Alaska. Tongass Narrows is Ketchikan's "main street" and is used by cruise ships, commercial tugs, fishing boats and floatplanes.

**transom:** transom seat; a kind of bench seat, usually with a locker or drawers underneath.

**twenty-five** or **.25:** a small handgun chambered for the .25 ACP (Automatic Colt Pistol) cartridge designed by American firearms inventor John M. Browning (1855–1926).

**Uncle Sam:** the cartoon embodiment of the government of the United States of America beginning in the first part of the nineteenth century. The initials US, of Uncle Sam, were also taken to stand for "United States."

**well deck:** space on the main deck of a ship lying at a lower level between the bridge and either a raised forward deck or a raised deck at the stern that usually has cabins underneath.

# L. Ron Hubbard
# in the Golden Age
# of Pulp Fiction

*In writing an adventure story
a writer has to know that he is adventuring
for a lot of people who cannot.
The writer has to take them here and there
about the globe and show them
excitement and love and realism.
As long as that writer is living the part of an
adventurer when he is hammering
the keys, he is succeeding with his story.*

*Adventuring is a state of mind.
If you adventure through life, you have a
good chance to be a success on paper.*

*Adventure doesn't mean globe-trotting,
exactly, and it doesn't mean great deeds.
Adventuring is like art.
You have to live it to make it real.*

*—L. RON HUBBARD*

# L. Ron Hubbard
# and American
# Pulp Fiction

B ORN March 13, 1911, L. Ron Hubbard lived a life at least as expansive as the stories with which he enthralled a hundred million readers through a fifty-year career.

Originally hailing from Tilden, Nebraska, he spent his formative years in a classically rugged Montana, replete with the cowpunchers, lawmen and desperadoes who would later people his Wild West adventures. And lest anyone imagine those adventures were drawn from vicarious experience, he was not only breaking broncs at a tender age, he was also among the few whites ever admitted into Blackfoot society as a bona fide blood brother. While if only to round out an otherwise rough and tumble youth, his mother was that rarity of her time—a thoroughly educated woman—who introduced her son to the classics of Occidental literature even before his seventh birthday.

But as any dedicated L. Ron Hubbard reader will attest, his world extended far beyond Montana. In point of fact, and as the son of a United States naval officer, by the age of eighteen he had traveled over a quarter of a million miles. Included therein were three Pacific crossings to a then still mysterious Asia, where he ran with the likes of Her British Majesty's agent-in-place

*L. Ron Hubbard, left, at Congressional Airport, Washington, DC, 1931, with members of George Washington University flying club.*

for North China, and the last in the line of Royal Magicians from the court of Kublai Khan. For the record, L. Ron Hubbard was also among the first Westerners to gain admittance to forbidden Tibetan monasteries below Manchuria, and his photographs of China's Great Wall long graced American geography texts.

Upon his return to the United States and a hasty completion of his interrupted high school education, the young Ron Hubbard entered George Washington University. There, as fans of his aerial adventures may have heard, he earned his wings as a pioneering barnstormer at the dawn of American aviation. He also earned a place in free-flight record books for the longest sustained flight above Chicago. Moreover, as a roving reporter for *Sportsman Pilot* (featuring his first professionally penned articles), he further helped inspire a generation of pilots who would take America to world airpower.

Immediately beyond his sophomore year, Ron embarked on the first of his famed ethnological expeditions, initially to then untrammeled Caribbean shores (descriptions of which would later fill a whole series of West Indies mystery-thrillers). That the Puerto Rican interior would also figure into the future of Ron Hubbard stories was likewise no accident. For in addition to cultural studies of the island, a 1932–33

LRH expedition is rightly remembered as conducting the first complete mineralogical survey of a Puerto Rico under United States jurisdiction.

There was many another adventure along this vein: As a lifetime member of the famed Explorers Club, L. Ron Hubbard charted North Pacific waters with the first shipboard radio direction finder, and so pioneered a long-range navigation system universally employed until the late twentieth century. While not to put too fine an edge on it, he also held a rare Master Mariner's license to pilot any vessel, of any tonnage in any ocean.

Yet lest we stray too far afield, there is an LRH note at this juncture in his saga, and it reads in part:

*"I started out writing for the pulps, writing the best I knew, writing for every mag on the stands, slanting as well as I could."*

To which one might add: His earliest submissions date from the summer of 1934, and included tales drawn from true-to-life Asian adventures, with characters roughly modeled on British/American intelligence operatives he had known in Shanghai. His early Westerns were similarly peppered with details drawn from personal experience. Although therein lay a first hard lesson from the often cruel world of the pulps. His first Westerns were soundly rejected as lacking the authenticity of a Max Brand yarn

*Capt. L. Ron Hubbard in Ketchikan, Alaska, 1940, on his Alaskan Radio Experimental Expedition, the first of three voyages conducted under the Explorers Club flag.*

(a particularly frustrating comment given L. Ron Hubbard's Westerns came straight from his Montana homeland, while Max Brand was a mediocre New York poet named Frederick Schiller Faust, who turned out implausible six-shooter tales from the terrace of an Italian villa).

Nevertheless, and needless to say, L. Ron Hubbard persevered and soon earned a reputation as among the most publishable names in pulp fiction, with a ninety percent placement rate of first-draft manuscripts. He was also among the most prolific, averaging between seventy and a hundred thousand words a month. Hence the rumors that L. Ron Hubbard had redesigned a typewriter for faster keyboard action and pounded out manuscripts on a continuous roll of butcher paper to save the precious seconds it took to insert a single sheet of paper into manual typewriters of the day.

That all L. Ron Hubbard stories did not run beneath said byline is yet another aspect of pulp fiction lore. That is, as publishers periodically rejected manuscripts from top-drawer authors if only to avoid paying top dollar, L. Ron Hubbard and company just as frequently replied with submissions under various pseudonyms. In Ron's case, the

---

**A MAN OF MANY NAMES**

*Between 1934 and 1950, L. Ron Hubbard authored more than fifteen million words of fiction in more than two hundred classic publications. To supply his fans and editors with stories across an array of genres and pulp titles, he adopted fifteen pseudonyms in addition to his already renowned L. Ron Hubbard byline.*

*Winchester Remington Colt*
*Lt. Jonathan Daly*
*Capt. Charles Gordon*
*Capt. L. Ron Hubbard*
*Bernard Hubbel*
*Michael Keith*
*Rene Lafayette*
*Legionnaire 148*
*Legionnaire 14830*
*Ken Martin*
*Scott Morgan*
*Lt. Scott Morgan*
*Kurt von Rachen*
*Barry Randolph*
*Capt. Humbert Reynolds*

---

list included: Rene Lafayette, Captain Charles Gordon, Lt. Scott Morgan and the notorious Kurt von Rachen—supposedly on the lam for a murder rap, while hammering out two-fisted prose in Argentina. The point: While L. Ron Hubbard as Ken Martin spun stories of Southeast Asian intrigue, LRH as Barry Randolph authored tales of

*L. Ron Hubbard, circa 1930, at the outset of a literary career that would finally span half a century.*

romance on the Western range—which, stretching between a dozen genres is how he came to stand among the two hundred elite authors providing close to a million tales through the glory days of American Pulp Fiction.

In evidence of exactly that, by 1936 L. Ron Hubbard was literally leading pulp fiction's elite as president of New York's American Fiction Guild. Members included a veritable pulp hall of fame: Lester "Doc Savage" Dent, Walter "The Shadow" Gibson, and the legendary Dashiell Hammett—to cite but a few.

Also in evidence of just where L. Ron Hubbard stood within his first two years on the American pulp circuit: By the spring of 1937, he was ensconced in Hollywood, adopting a Caribbean thriller for Columbia Pictures, remembered today as *The Secret of Treasure Island*. Comprising fifteen thirty-minute episodes, the L. Ron Hubbard screenplay led to the most profitable matinée serial in Hollywood history. In accord with Hollywood culture, he was thereafter continually called upon

*The 1937* Secret of Treasure Island, *a fifteen-episode serial adapted for the screen by L. Ron Hubbard from his novel,* Murder at Pirate Castle.

to rewrite/doctor scripts—most famously for long-time friend and fellow adventurer Clark Gable.

In the interim—and herein lies another distinctive chapter of the L. Ron Hubbard story—he continually worked to open Pulp Kingdom gates to up-and-coming authors. Or, for that matter, anyone who wished to write. It was a fairly unconventional stance, as markets were already thin and competition razor sharp. But the fact remains, it was an L. Ron Hubbard hallmark that he vehemently lobbied on behalf of young authors—regularly supplying instructional articles to trade journals, guest-lecturing to short story classes at George Washington University and Harvard, and even founding his own creative writing competition. It was established in 1940, dubbed the Golden Pen, and guaranteed winners both New York representation and publication in *Argosy*.

But it was John W. Campbell Jr.'s *Astounding Science Fiction* that finally proved the most memorable LRH vehicle. While every fan of L. Ron Hubbard's galactic epics undoubtedly knows the story, it nonetheless bears repeating: By late 1938, the pulp publishing magnate of Street & Smith was determined to revamp *Astounding Science Fiction* for broader readership. In particular, senior editorial director F. Orlin Tremaine called for stories with a stronger *human element*. When acting editor John W. Campbell balked, preferring his spaceship-driven tales, Tremaine enlisted Hubbard. Hubbard, in turn, replied with the genre's first truly *character-driven* works, wherein heroes are pitted not against bug-eyed monsters but the mystery and majesty of deep space itself—and thus was launched the Golden Age of Science Fiction.

The names alone are enough to quicken the pulse of any science fiction aficionado, including LRH friend and protégé, Robert Heinlein, Isaac Asimov, A. E. van Vogt and Ray Bradbury. Moreover, when coupled with LRH stories of fantasy, we further come to what's rightly been described as the foundation of every modern tale of horror: L. Ron Hubbard's immortal *Fear*. It was rightly proclaimed by Stephen King as one of the very few works to genuinely warrant that overworked term "classic"—as in: *"This is a classic tale of creeping, surreal menace and horror. . . . This is one of the really, really good ones."*

L. Ron Hubbard, 1948, among fellow science fiction luminaries at the World Science Fiction Convention in Toronto.

To accommodate the greater body of L. Ron Hubbard fantasies, Street & Smith inaugurated *Unknown*—a classic pulp if there ever was one, and wherein readers were soon thrilling to the likes of *Typewriter in the Sky* and *Slaves of Sleep* of which Frederik Pohl would declare: *"There are bits and pieces from Ron's work that became part of the language in ways that very few other writers managed."*

And, indeed, at J. W. Campbell Jr.'s insistence, Ron was regularly drawing on themes from the Arabian Nights and so introducing readers to a world of genies, jinn, Aladdin and Sinbad—all of which, of course, continue to float through cultural mythology to this day.

At least as influential in terms of post-apocalypse stories was L. Ron Hubbard's 1940 *Final Blackout*. Generally acclaimed as the finest anti-war novel of the decade and among the ten best works of the genre ever authored—here, too, was a tale that would live on in ways few other writers imagined.

Hence, the later Robert Heinlein verdict: "Final Blackout *is as perfect a piece of science fiction as has ever been written."*

Like many another who both lived and wrote American pulp adventure, the war proved a tragic end to Ron's sojourn in the pulps. He served with distinction in four theaters and was highly decorated for commanding corvettes in the North Pacific. He was also grievously wounded in combat, lost many a close friend and colleague and thus resolved to say farewell to pulp fiction and devote himself to what it had supported these many years—namely, his serious research.

*Portland, Oregon, 1943; L. Ron Hubbard, captain of the US Navy subchaser PC 815.*

But in no way was the LRH literary saga at an end, for as he wrote some thirty years later, in 1980:

*"Recently there came a period when I had little to do. This was novel in a life so crammed with busy years, and I decided to amuse myself by writing a novel that was pure science fiction."*

That work was *Battlefield Earth: A Saga of the Year 3000*. It was an immediate *New York Times* bestseller and, in fact, the first international science fiction blockbuster in decades. It was not, however, L. Ron Hubbard's magnum opus, as that distinction is generally reserved for his next and final work: The 1.2 million word *Mission Earth*.

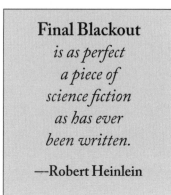

**Final Blackout**
*is as perfect a piece of science fiction as has ever been written.*

—Robert Heinlein

How he managed those 1.2 million words in just over twelve months is yet another piece of the L. Ron Hubbard legend. But the fact remains, he did indeed author a ten-volume *dekalogy* that lives in publishing history for the fact that each and every volume of the series was also a *New York Times* bestseller.

Moreover, as subsequent generations discovered L. Ron Hubbard through republished works and novelizations of his screenplays, the mere fact of his name on a cover signaled an international bestseller. . . . Until, to date, sales of his works exceed hundreds of millions, and he otherwise remains among the most enduring and widely read authors in literary history. Although as a final word on the tales of L. Ron Hubbard, perhaps it's enough to simply reiterate what editors told readers in the glory days of American Pulp Fiction:

*He writes the way he does, brothers, because he's been there, seen it and done it!*

# THE STORIES FROM THE
# GOLDEN AGE

Your ticket to adventure starts here with the Stories from
the Golden Age collection by master storyteller L. Ron Hubbard.
These gripping tales are set in a kaleidoscope of exotic locales and brim
with fascinating characters, including some of the
most vile villains, dangerous dames and brazen heroes
you'll ever get to meet.

The entire collection of over one hundred and fifty stories is being
released in a series of eighty books and audiobooks.
For an up-to-date listing of available titles,
go to www.goldenagestories.com.

## AIR ADVENTURE

## FAR-FLUNG ADVENTURE

## SEA ADVENTURE

## TALES FROM THE ORIENT

*The Devil—With Wings*    *Pearl Pirate*
*The Falcon Killer*    *The Red Dragon*
*Five Mex for a Million*    *Spy Killer*
*Golden Hell*    *Tah*
*The Green God*    *The Trail of the Red Diamonds*
*Hurricane's Roar*    *Wind-Gone-Mad*
*Inky Odds*    *Yellow Loot*
*Orders Is Orders*

## MYSTERY

*The Blow Torch Murder*    *The Grease Spot*
*Brass Keys to Murder*    *Killer Ape*
*Calling Squad Cars!*    *Killer's Law*
*The Carnival of Death*    *The Mad Dog Murder*
*The Chee-Chalker*    *Mouthpiece*
*Dead Men Kill*    *Murder Afloat*
*The Death Flyer*    *The Slickers*
*Flame City*    *They Killed Him Dead*

119

## FANTASY

Borrowed Glory
The Crossroads
Danger in the Dark
The Devil's Rescue
He Didn't Like Cats

If I Were You
The Last Drop
The Room
The Tramp

## SCIENCE FICTION

The Automagic Horse
Battle of Wizards
Battling Bolto
The Beast
Beyond All Weapons
A Can of Vacuum
The Conroy Diary
The Dangerous Dimension
Final Enemy
The Great Secret
Greed
The Invaders

A Matter of Matter
The Obsolete Weapon
One Was Stubborn
The Planet Makers
The Professor Was a Thief
The Slaver
Space Can
Strain
Tough Old Man
240,000 Miles Straight Up
When Shadows Fall

## WESTERN

121

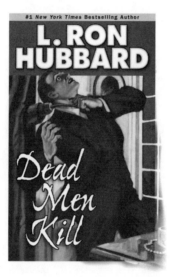

# JOIN THE PULP REVIVAL
## *America in the 1930s and 40s*

Pulp fiction was in its heyday and 30 million readers were regularly riveted by the larger-than-life tales of master storyteller L. Ron Hubbard. For this was pulp fiction's golden age, when the writing was raw and every page packed a walloping punch.

That magic can now be yours. An evocative world of nefarious villains, exotic intrigues, courageous heroes and heroines—a world that today's cinema has barely tapped for tales of adventure and swashbucklers.

Enroll today in the Stories from the Golden Age Club and begin receiving your monthly feature edition selected from more than 150 stories in the collection.

You may choose to enjoy them as either a paperback or audiobook for the special membership price of $9.95 each month along with FREE shipping and handling.

CALL TOLL-FREE: 1-877-8GALAXY
(1-877-842-5299) OR GO ONLINE TO
**www.goldenagestories.com**
AND BECOME PART OF THE PULP REVIVAL!

Prices are set in US dollars only. For non-US residents, please call
1-323-466-7815 for pricing information. Free shipping available for US residents only.

Galaxy Press, 7051 Hollywood Blvd., Suite 200, Hollywood, CA 90028